"Who Does The Mob Think Justin's Father Is?" Michael Asked.

"You," Heather told him.

Yes, him. Who else could it be? He was Heather's only lover, the only man she'd ever given herself to.

"You have no right to ask this of me. To expect me to raise your brother's son," Michael said.

"I'm not expecting you to do it forever. Just for a few months."

"Why didn't you think about me before you got tangled up in this mess?"

"Please understand. This is about Justin. An innocent child."

What the hell was he supposed to do? Let the mob take the boy away from her?

"Please." She went to the baby and picked him up.

Michael frowned, and Justin took that moment to smile.

Damn. Damn. Damn.

"All right," he said as the boy's grin tunneled an unwelcome path straight into his cautious, it'll-be-over-in-two-months heart.

Dear Reader,

Experience passion and power in six brand-new, provocative titles from Silhouette Desire this July!

Begin with *Scenes of Passion* (#1519) by *New York Times* bestselling author Suzanne Brockmann. In this scintillating love story, a pretend marriage turned all too real reveals the torrid emotions and secrets of a former bad-boy millionaire and his prim heiress.

DYNASTIES: THE BARONES continues in July with *Cinderella's Millionaire* (#1520) by Katherine Garbera, in which a pretty pastry cook's red-hot passion melts the defenses of a brooding Barone hero. *In Bed with the Enemy,* (#1521) by rising star Kathie DeNosky, is the second LONE STAR COUNTRY CLUB title in Desire. In this installment, a lady agent and her lone-wolf counterpart bump more than heads during an investigation into a gun-smuggling ring.

What would you do if you were *Expecting the Cowboy's Baby* (#1522)? Discover how a plain-Jane bookkeeper deals with this dilemma in this steamy love story, the second Silhouette Desire title by popular Harlequin Historicals author Charlene Sands. Then see how a brokenhearted rancher struggles to forgive the woman who betrayed him, in *Cherokee Dad* (#1523) by Sheri WhiteFeather. And in *The Gentrys: Cal* (#1524) by Linda Conrad, a wounded stock-car driver finds healing love in the arms of a sexy, mysterious nurse, and the Gentry siblings at last learn the truth about their parents' disappearance.

Beat the summer heat with these six new love stories from Silhouette Desire.

Enjoy!

Melissa Jeglinski
Senior Editor, Silhouette Desire

Please address questions and book requests to:
Silhouette Reader Service
U.S.: 3010 Walden Ave., P.O. Box 1325, Buffalo, NY 14269
Canadian: P.O. Box 609, Fort Erie, Ont. L2A 5X3

Cherokee Dad
SHERI WHITEFEATHER

Published by Silhouette Books
America's Publisher of Contemporary Romance

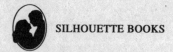

SILHOUETTE BOOKS

ISBN 0-373-76523-1

CHEROKEE DAD

Printed in U.S.A.

Books by Sheri WhiteFeather

Silhouette Desire

Warrior's Baby #1248
Skyler Hawk: Lone Brave #1272
Jesse Hawk: Brave Father #1278
Cheyenne Dad #1300
Night Wind's Woman #1332
Tycoon Warrior #1364
Cherokee #1376
Comanche Vow #1388
Cherokee Marriage Dare #1478
Sleeping with Her Rival #1496
Cherokee Baby #1509
Cherokee Dad #1523

SHERI WHITEFEATHER

lives in Southern California and enjoys ethnic dining, attending powwows and visiting art galleries and vintage clothing stores near the beach. Since her one true passion is writing, she is thrilled to be a part of the Silhouette Desire line. When she isn't writing, she often reads until the wee hours of the morning.

Sheri's husband, a member of the Muscogee Creek Nation, inspires many of her stories. They have a son, a daughter and a trio of cats—domestic and wild. She loves to hear from her readers. You may write to her at: P.O. Box 17146, Anaheim, California 92817. Visit her Web site at www.SheriWhiteFeather.com.

To my editor, Melissa "MJ" Jeglinski, for truly caring about my work and giving me the opportunity to spread my wings. And to Joan Marlow Golan and Tara Gavin for trusting me to revise the proposal after they bought it. This isn't the only Mafia-driven book I've written. Silhouette planted the seed in their Lone Star Country Club series, allowing me to let it sprout in a few different directions. I spent some engaging years in L.A., and I couldn't resist creating a Los Angeles-based mob.

One

Rain slashed against the windows, and lightning flashed in white-hot streaks. The intermittent bursts of thunder reminded twenty-five-year-old Michael Elk of the Cherokee thunder beings his uncle had told him about.

As a youth, Michael had scoffed at the existence of those revered beings, but on this weather-ravaged night, he wondered if they were out there, sanctioned by the Creator to perform special duties.

Thunderous duties.

Boom! Boom! Boom!

Another pounding nearly jarred him out of his skin.

He placed the beer he'd been nursing on a side table and told himself to get a grip. Watching an old Hitchcock movie and listening to the storm was no reason to panic.

Then why did he sense that something was about

to happen? Something, he decided, as he stared at the TV, that wasn't in the script.

Another thunderous noise slammed through the living room, and Michael looked around, just to reassure himself that everything was all right.

He lived in a red-and-white farmhouse in the Texas Hill Country, the place where he'd been born. A place that gave him peace, at least most of the time.

Boom! Boom! Boom!

Again, that sound. It seemed too close, too personal, too—

Too much like someone banging on the door?

Cursing his stupidity, he rose. Then wondered if thunder beings ever came to a man's door.

Oh, sure. Right along with the Easter Bunny, Freddy Kruger and the Tooth Fairy.

Or maybe Santa Claus in a Halloween mask.

With an amused chuckle, he opened the door.

And flinched as if he'd been sucker punched.

Heather Richmond stood on the other side, dripping with rain and hugging a blanketed bundle to her chest.

Heather—his missing girlfriend, the woman who'd purposely disappeared a year and a half ago; the stunning blonde who'd sent his tortured heart to hell.

Their gazes locked, and his pulse jumped to his throat. Water glistened on her cheeks and dotted her lashes. Even in the dark, her eyes shined bright and blue.

"I tried the bell," she said, her voice quiet amid the storm. "But it wasn't working."

He could only stare, could only struggle to get his emotions in check. The cumbersome bundle in her arms looked suspiciously like a baby.

Whose baby? His or someone else's?

He had no idea what Heather had been up to. She'd gone to California on a business trip, then vanished into thin air. He'd filed a missing person's report, frantic something horrible had happened to her, but a police investigation had turned up deceitful evidence.

"May I come in?" she asked.

He wanted to say no, to send her away. But the blanket moved and a little hand popped out from the damp folds of the fluffy material.

He couldn't send the child away, not if it was his.

Without speaking, he stepped back, allowing her entrance into the home they'd once shared.

She walked into the living room, making damp marks on the hardwood floor. When she adjusted the sleeping baby, he noticed a cap of dark hair.

"Michael?"

His name on her lips pierced him like an arrow. And so did memories of the police report. The convention Heather had supposedly attended never existed, and she'd closed her savings account in Los Angeles, withdrawing the money she'd acquired from her deceased mother's life insurance policy.

The LAPD concluded that she'd disappeared purposely, and since she hadn't been involved in a crime, they hadn't pursued her whereabouts.

There had been one vital clue in the mystery, though. The authorities discovered that Reed Blackwood, her half brother, had been living in L.A. and had left town on the day Heather closed her savings account.

But Reed was no longer on probation, so the ex-con was free to go where he pleased. And so, they'd claimed, was Heather.

Michael had considered hiring a private investigator to track her down, but his pride had gotten in the way. Why search for a woman who'd lied to him? Who'd gone to L.A. on a farce? Who'd stomped on his heart?

"Michael?" she said his name again, drawing his attention back to her.

"Yes?"

"Is it all right if we stay here tonight?"

We. Her and the child.

"Yes," he responded again.

After that, silence stretched between them. The air grew thick and tense, swirling like a poltergeist. Was she going to tell him about the baby? Offer him an explanation? Or would silence prevail, trapping him in this haunting lull?

Finally she spoke, her voice much too soft. "Will you bring in the baby's crib? It's a portable model. There's a small suitcase I need, too. And a diaper bag."

How old was the child? he wondered as he accepted Heather's keys and ventured outside. He'd yet to get a closer look, to determine its age.

Had she been carrying his babe in her womb when she'd run off?

The storm blasted his face, and he squinted into the rain. He suspected Heather's car was a rental since she'd left her other vehicle behind when she'd split.

He hauled in the requested items, and she thanked him quietly.

Silence again. Then, "Will you hold him while I make up his bed?"

Him. So the child was a boy.

Michael stepped forward, and she transferred the baby into his arms. He wasn't unfamiliar with babies;

his uncle had a six-week-old son. Of course, this child was bigger, much heavier than his tiny cousin.

The top of the blanket fell away, exposing golden skin, chubby cheeks and long sweeping lashes. He was a pretty baby, almost too pretty to be a boy.

"What's his name?" Michael asked.

She fluffed the bedding. "Justin."

He glanced at the child's face. He could see that Justin had some Indian blood in him. "How old is he, Heather?"

"Ten months." A little nervously, she reached for the baby and placed him in the crib, removing the blanket that swaddled him.

Justin stirred but didn't waken.

A ten-month-old with Indian blood. It didn't take a genius to do the math, to figure the ethnic equation. "Is he mine?"

She didn't answer. Instead she fussed with the child's pajamas and adjusted a loose sock, fitting it back onto his foot.

Michael moved closer, anxious, hopeful, afraid. "I asked you if he's mine."

She covered the baby, and the boy rolled onto his side. When she stood, her eyes, those incredible blue eyes, met Michael's. She still wore an overcoat, and her waist-length hair was sprinkled with rain.

"Heather?" he persisted.

Rather than respond, she turned away. As she headed out the door, Michael followed her, wondering what the hell was up.

They stood on the porch, rain blowing toward them.

"We can't talk inside. Not until I sweep the house for bugs."

Bugs? Michael stared at her. He knew she meant electronic devices. "What's going on? What kind of trouble are you in?"

"Reed's in trouble."

He shook his head. Her brother always was. "And what about the boy? Is he mine?"

"Justin is Reed's son."

Michael's stomach dropped. The baby wasn't his.

Damn Heather all to hell. She'd brought her brother's child to his house. The man he'd forbade her to see. The ex-con he'd banned from their lives.

Of course Justin looked as if he had Indian blood, Reed was half-Cherokee, just like Michael.

"Who's his mother?"

"Her name is Beverly."

"So where in the hell is she? And Reed for that matter? What are you doing with their kid, Heather?"

Her breath hitched. "It's a long story."

"Yeah, well, I've got plenty of time."

Heather couldn't explain, not now. She gestured to the storm, to the blinding rain. "It's pouring out. I'm cold and tired."

And afraid.

Fearful of how to tell Michael her story without revealing the secret that would keep him from ever forgiving her.

Already she could see pain and anger in his eyes. She'd never meant to hurt him. He was, and always would be, the man she loved. But she couldn't turn her back on her brother, not even for Michael. So she'd gone to California.

Then her entire world had turned inside out.

Heather drew a shaky breath. What if Michael uncovered her secret on his own? Was that possible?

No, she told herself. That wouldn't happen. The only person who could spill her secret was Dr. Mills and the kindly old physician wouldn't betray Heather's medical files.

Would he?

Michael spiked a hand through his shoulder-length hair, and Heather couldn't help but study him. He wore a black T-shirt, threadbare jeans and scuffed boots. He'd always been tough. Dashing yet dangerous.

A renegade.

Just like Reed. At one time, her half-Cherokee brother and her half-Cherokee lover had been boyhood friends, running wild and cheating the law.

Two years their junior, she used to follow them around, worried about Reed and smitten by Michael. He'd always smiled at her, even when she was a bony, flat-chested little girl.

She lifted her gaze and slammed into his.

He wasn't smiling now.

"Michael?"

"What?" he snapped.

"Don't use the phone or tell anyone I'm here. No one, not even your uncle."

"For how long?"

"Until I secure your house."

"If your brother dragged me into something illegal, I'm going to kill him."

Would he think protecting a child's life was criminal?

He squinted through a gust of rain. "I should make you tell me. I should demand the whole damn story out of you. Right here. Right now. But I won't. And do you know why?"

Nervous, she shook her head. He sounded so cold, so hard.

"Because another day won't matter. What's done is done. You made your choice when you lied to me. When you didn't call. Didn't come back."

"I'm sorry," she said, willing herself not to cry, not to break down in front of him.

Would he understand once she told him why she didn't call? Why she didn't come back before now?

Tough and terse, Michael shrugged away her apology, and she banked the tears flooding her eyes.

They went back inside and Heather removed her coat, fearful of what tomorrow would bring. Would Michael agree to help her and Justin? Or was her fate doomed?

As close as she and Michael had been, he'd never actually told her that he loved her, not even when he'd asked her to live with him.

But, then, no one except Heather's wayward brother had ever said those words. Reed's "Thanks for caring," and "I love you, kiddo," had been her lifeline, the hope that she was truly worthy of being loved.

Heather hadn't been able to count on her parents, not her stern, critical father or her nervous, flighty mother.

She'd promised Reed that she would give his son more than what they'd had. More kindness. More affection. More love.

And Reed understood that well. Her father, who'd been her brother's disapproving stepfather, had punished Reed at every turn, raising his fists until Reed grew tall enough to fight back.

She knelt to smooth the baby's thick brown hair, then looked up at Michael.

He shifted his feet. He seemed so dark, so menacing. Yet she recalled how gentle he could be, how tender, how boyish and playful.

He used to tickle her, attack her ribs until she nearly died laughing. Then he'd kiss her until she sighed his name and melted onto the bed, his naked body covering hers.

"You can sleep in the guest room," he offered, although his tone lacked hospitality.

"Thank you, but the couch is fine. Justin's bed is already made up out here, and I'd like to be near him."

Without speaking, he went to the linen closet, returned with a burgundy quilt and a mismatched pillow, stacking them hastily on the sofa.

His house was cluttered, but he'd never kept things tidy. Heather had picked up after him, but it was her nature to keep order, to organize everything but her love-starved heart.

"I'll see you in the morning," she said.

He glanced at the baby, then brought his gaze back to her. "There's milk in the fridge if you need it."

"Thank you." She watched him snap off the TV and walk down the hall.

Copper-skinned, raven-haired Michael Elk. The man she loved. The man she wished she hadn't betrayed.

Michael dragged himself into the shower. He'd tossed and turned most of the night. Eventually he'd succumbed to exhaustion, only to discover he'd overslept.

After the water pummeled his body and he reached for a towel, he told himself to relax, to confront the day with as much patience as he could muster.

As he brushed his teeth, he noticed another toothbrush on the counter.

Heather's.

The past had come back to taunt him, the bittersweet memories of living with her, of sharing the same space. Michael's old farmhouse had three bedrooms and one cozy bath.

He rinsed his mouth and stole a second glance at her toothbrush, struggling with the unwelcome intimacy it stirred.

Finally he threw on some jeans and a work shirt, then headed to the kitchen to start a pot of coffee.

But she'd beat him to it. An aromatic brew was already perking. He poured himself a cup and stood quietly for a moment, trying to stabilize his heart. Then he entered the living room and stumbled straight into a network of electronic equipment.

The countersurveillance system on the coffee table appeared to be running in an automatic mode as Heather utilized another detector Reed had probably built.

Her brother was a young, cocky genius, as skilled as someone with a Ph.D. in electrical engineering, and he must have taught her what she needed to know.

The device seemed fairly simple to operate, but that didn't mean it wasn't effective. Reed Blackwood didn't build spy shop gadgets. He dealt in the real thing.

The baby made a noise, drawing Michael's attention to the crib. Justin was asleep, but a telltale bottle of milk lay at his side. Apparently he'd drunk some nourishment and drifted off again.

Just then Heather turned to look at Michael, to meet his gaze.

Her long, white-blond hair fell in dazzling disarray, and she wore a simple, sky-blue blouse and slim-fitting jeans. She moistened her lips, and at that sexually charged instant, she reminded him of Eve—the temptress Adam couldn't resist.

Well, I'm not Adam, he thought. He wasn't about to bite the proverbial apple.

"Good morning," she said.

"Yeah." He flicked his head like a hot-blooded stallion, and then made a sardonic toast with his coffee. "'Morning."

Ignoring the sarcasm, she adjusted the detector. She'd been in the process of sweeping an old rolltop desk and every item on it.

"When do you have to be to work?" she asked.

"When I feel like it." She knew damn well that he kept his own hours. He and his uncle ran a prestigious guest ranch in the hills, but Michael didn't punch a time clock.

And neither did she, for that matter. She used to be the events coordinator at the ranch, a position she'd more or less dumped on his lap.

As he drank coffee that failed to warm his belly, she continued the sweep.

She carted her equipment into his bedroom, and he realized it was the only room she hadn't scanned. Apparently she'd been up since the crack of dawn, making her inspection.

Michael remained in the living room. The idea that his house needed debugging made him queasy. He didn't want to envision strangers eavesdropping on his life, invading his privacy—the times he cursed to himself, mumbled at the TV, punched walls out of sheer frustration.

All because of Heather.

He watched the baby sleep and finished his coffee. It wasn't strong enough, but the caffeine helped nonetheless.

By the time Heather returned, he'd brewed a second pot. He considered a cigarette, and then reconsidered. He supposed lighting up near the kid wouldn't be right.

"I didn't find anything." She sat on the sofa and placed her coffee on the end table. "But I can't be sure about your phones. I don't have the skills to detect a sophisticated wiretap or bug."

"Your brother didn't teach you?" he asked, unable to curb the bite in his tone.

She sighed. "A wiretap can be installed several miles from the target location. And a radio transmitter can be hidden eighteen feet in the air."

"So what do we do?"

"Don't discuss sensitive issues on the phone."

Michael narrowed his eyes. "That's it?"

"No. I have the number of an old friend of Reed's. Someone he trusts. He's a communications expert. He'll check the lines. I'm not sure when, though."

"Fine. Whatever." Michael was tired of the cloak and dagger, the spy game Reed had put her up to. He wanted answers.

Now.

"Talk," he said. "Tell me what's going on."

Her competent hands turned shaky. "The reason I left?"

He steeled his gaze. "And stayed away so long."

"Of course, yes. You deserve to know the truth."

Michael frowned. Had she whispered the word truth? Or was it his imagination? She had spoken quietly as it was.

"Anytime you're ready," he prodded.

She turned toward the window. The unexpected storm had passed, Michael noticed, but rain still drizzled. The sound mingled softly with the baby's gentle breathing.

"Reed called me from California," she said. "He'd been secretly dating a girl named Beverly, a college student from a wealthy family, and he wanted to marry her."

Michael raised his eyebrows at that, but he kept his mouth shut, letting her continue.

"Beverly's father threatened Reed. He warned him to stay away from his daughter. So Reed and Beverly were planning to skip town, to elope and disappear for good." Heather shifted, facing him again. "I assumed her father was a politician or a powerful law enforcement official, someone who could find a way to frame Reed for a crime he didn't commit. To send him back to prison."

Yeah, right. As if Reed needed an excuse to get locked up again, to thumb his nose at society. Michael used to run around with Heather's brother, creating small-town havoc like the cigarette-stealing, whiskey-rousing, gambling-behind-the-barn delinquents they'd been. Only Reed had eventually taken his crimes to adult levels. He'd celebrated his high school graduation by robbing the principal's house. He'd done it as a lark, as a kiss-my-ass rush, but he'd carved out his future just the same.

Reed's next crime had involved a little more danger. And the one after that had landed him a short but memorable prison term.

The baby awakened with a fierce cry, interrupting Michael's thoughts.

Heather dashed up and rushed to the boy's aid. Lifting him in her arms, she cradled him, soothing him with maternal whispers.

Justin quieted immediately. He put his head on her shoulder and made a contented sound.

Michael did his damnedest to ignore the tenderness between woman and child. He was already emotional over Heather, and getting sappy over Reed's kid would only make matters worse.

"I need to change him and give him his lunch," she said.

Michael waved his hand, feigning indifference. "Go ahead."

She dressed Justin in a blue T-shirt, a fresh diaper, snap-up jeans and a bib. He wiggled and squirmed and made excited noises.

She kept him on her lap as she fed him, but Michael could see that it wasn't an easy task. He knew there was a high chair in her trunk, but he suspected she didn't want to burden him to bring it in.

Justin said "um" after every bite. Did that mean yum? Michael couldn't imagine that the kid actually thought mushy veggies and jarred meat were yummy.

As Heather wiped his messy face, he scrunched his nose in disapproval, then squealed after he was clean. Next he drank from a bottle, tipping it himself.

When Justin looked curiously at Michael, Heather followed the boy's gaze. Michael shifted in his chair, wishing the scrutinizing would end.

Finally, it did.

She placed Justin back in the portable crib, which apparently doubled as a playpen. A handful of toys followed him into the little cage.

It wasn't a very fancy cage, Michael noticed. Although clean, it appeared old, possibly purchased from a secondhand store.

"Tell me the rest of the story," he said, suddenly feeling bad for the kid. He remembered surviving on hand-me-downs, at least until his wealthy uncle had showed up.

Heather drew a breath. "I wanted to say goodbye to Reed in person. To see him before he vanished. He told me that once he and Beverly took off, he wouldn't be able to contact me again."

So she'd arranged a bogus trip to L.A., Michael thought. Allowing him to believe she was attending a conference. "You weren't supposed to keep in touch with Reed to begin with. You promised me that you'd cut him out your life, that you'd stay away from him."

"I know, but I couldn't. Not this time."

Not anytime, he realized. She'd been secretly conversing with Reed all along.

"When I arrived in L.A., all hell broke lose. I went straight to my brother's downtown loft and found Beverly there, crying over Reed. He was on the floor, unconscious. He'd been severely beaten. A warning from Beverly's father to stay away from her."

Justin made a humming sound as he stacked colorful blocks. When they fell, he laughed and clapped, unaware of the distress in Heather's voice.

"I tried to dial 911," she went on to say. "But Beverly begged me not to, even though Reed was a bruised and bloodied mess. I didn't know what to do.'' She paused, as if recalling her terror. ''Then Beverly asked me to help her get him out of town. To tend to his injuries.''

''And that's what you did?''

''Yes, but the ordeal didn't stop there.''

''What ordeal?''

''We ended up on the run.''

''From who? Beverly's father?''

''Yes.'' She looked up and met his gaze, her voice haunted. ''Her father isn't an ordinary man. He's—''

Frustrated, Michael moved to the edge of his seat. ''He's what?''

''An L.A. crime boss. We were on the run from the West Coast Family.''

As her words registered, Michael's heartbeat blasted his chest. ''You mean the mob?'' The guys who ran racketeering and extortion rings? Smuggled drugs? Pumped their enemies full of bullets?

''Yes,'' she answered quietly. ''The mob.''

Two

"I was trapped," Heather said, praying Michael would understand. "I couldn't contact you. I couldn't risk a phone call."

"You mean to tell me that Reed couldn't have scrambled your location, kept the mob from tracing the call?"

"Yes, but that wouldn't have been enough. The conversation still could have been bugged, even if the eavesdropper couldn't pinpoint where it was coming from."

"So?"

"So we had no idea what they'd do. The mob doesn't normally take hostages or harm innocent people, but this was different."

Unconvinced and much too macho, he squinted at her. "You were afraid they'd hurt me?"

"Or threaten someone close to you. Try to find out how much you knew."

His eyes narrowed even more. "They could have done that anyway."

"There'd be no need. Not unless they suspected you'd been in touch with me. That you were involved somehow. Maybe even helping Reed."

"So you let me suffer? Wonder where you were? Why you'd left?"

"Yes," she said. "It was the only thing I could do to ensure your safety."

He didn't respond, so she continued. "My brother was in severe danger. Not only was he trying to go straight, to end his affiliation with the mob, he'd fallen in love with the boss's daughter. That's a fatal combination."

"Where is Reed?" Michael asked.

Heather stole a glance at the baby, who amused himself with a musical pony. "He's still on the run."

"But you're here, with his son."

"Yes." She studied the pony. Reed had purchased it for Justin just weeks before he'd been born. It was the only toy the child owned that hadn't come from a thrift store.

There was another lullaby pony, she thought. Buried near a cabin in Oklahoma.

"Tell me about Justin's mother."

She reached for the bitter coffee Michael had brewed and took a sip, hoping to calm her quaking hands. She still dreamed about the other pony. Still cried sometimes in her sleep.

"Beverly wasn't doing well. She had a difficult pregnancy. I was concerned about the delivery, if there would be complications."

"Were there?"

"No. It was fine. A long labor, but fine."

Heather thought about the leather-wrapped bundle Reed had buried. The Cherokee prayers he'd chanted would remain forever in her mind, in her heart.

"But soon after Justin was born, Beverly became ill. She assumed it was stress. We were constantly on the move, and that took its toll on everyone."

How many states had they passed through? How many nights had they slept in their vehicle? Washed up at gas stations and launderettes? Jumped from campsite to campsite, living on the fish Reed caught? "Beverly got a cough that wouldn't go away. But no matter how fatigued she was, she refused to see a doctor."

"Why? Because she was afraid of drawing attention to herself?"

"Yes." She could still see Beverly, pale and tired, letting Heather care for her son on the days she couldn't manage him. "Reed did everything he could to convince her to see a doctor. But she was determined to get well on her own. To try homeopathic remedies."

Michael's voice turned hard. "What in the hell was Reed planning on doing? Being on the road forever?"

"He and Beverly had originally intended to go to Mexico, but Reed's contact in Mexico City said the mob was already searching for them there." She glanced at her hands, at her nervously chewed nails. "We had no idea where else they were searching. So we just kept running." Struggling to make the money last, she thought. Her brother taking day labor jobs when he could. Using fake IDs. Switching vehicles, registering them to an alias.

"So, who is Beverly's father? What's his name?"

"Denny Halloway. The FBI calls the West Coast Family the Hollywood mob. Halloway, Hollywood. It's a play on words, and he has connections in the entertainment industry."

Michael sighed. "I don't know anything about the Mafia. Other than what I've seen on TV. The Italian guys in New York. Or New Jersey or wherever."

"The West Coast Family isn't an Italian outfit." And Heather knew more about the Mafia than she'd ever dreamed possible. Reed had been a "made" man. He'd sacrificed his soul for organized crime. "My brother was working on a way to send me home. To fake his, Beverly's and Justin's deaths. To stage an accident where I was the only survivor. But Beverly got sick and everything changed."

"He should have sent all of you home. He shouldn't have kept two women and a baby on the run."

"Beverly didn't want to return to her family. She'd always detested what her father represented, the high-powered criminal lifestyle he led. Besides, she loved Reed and wanted to be with him. He was her husband. Her Cherokee husband," Heather clarified. "Reed performed a blanket ceremony. It wasn't legal, but it was binding."

Michael shook his head. "You wanted me to do that with you when you were sixteen. It was crazy."

Her chest constricted. "I was young and romantic. I wanted you to pledge yourself to me." To make a commitment, to swear off other girls and be with her, even though she wasn't of age. But he'd refused. He'd been an eighteen-year-old boy still sowing his sexual oats, still parading a slew of blondes through his bed.

They sat in silence for a while, caught in the past. Then Justin rose and held on to the edge of his crib, grinning at Heather, waving his pony with one hand, nearly losing his balance.

Refusing to cry, she smiled back at him. She had a child to raise, a son to consider. She had to stay strong.

"Did Beverly die?" Michael asked.

"No, but she probably won't live much longer. When she got worse, Reed insisted on taking her to a clinic. After a series of tests, they discovered she had small cell carcinoma of the lung, a rapidly progressing cancer. Without treatment, the median survival rate from diagnosis is only two to four months."

She continued to look at Justin. He was such a good baby, so easy to care for, so happy. Yet his mother was dying, and his father was running for his life.

"We made a decision. Beverly had to return to her family. She needed urgent medical care."

"I'm sorry," Michael said, sympathy lacing his voice.

Heather turned to study him, to absorb his sincerity. She knew his mother had died of cancer, that he'd watched her grow pale and weak. Just as she and Reed had watched Beverly deteriorate, without realizing the magnitude of her illness. "Beverly is only twenty-two. A nonsmoker. Lung cancer never occurred to us."

He merely nodded, a frown marring his brow. "Why didn't she take her son home with her?"

"She didn't want her father to have any part in raising him."

"And what about Reed?"

"He couldn't care for Justin, not living on the run. Reed knew that Beverly's father would never quit searching for him, that he'd always be a target. So they both decided to relinquish their child, to give him a chance for a clean, safe life."

And she remembered how devastated they'd been, how they'd held Justin and cried. They were losing each other and their baby. "We fabricated a lie. It was the only thing we could do. The only answer."

"What lie?" he asked, watching her through dark, penetrating eyes.

She glanced away, afraid those eyes could look into her soul and unmask her secrets. The other pony. The leather bundle. The Cherokee prayers.

"I was to become Justin's mother in every way," she said, still dodging his gaze. "Beverly wouldn't tell her family that she had a son. They didn't know that she was pregnant, and there were no hospital records, nothing that proved she'd given birth to him. He was born in a cabin in Oklahoma, with only Reed and I in attendance."

"And her father bought the lie? He never suspected that Justin was his grandson?"

"Why would he? Who would assume that a girl dying of cancer would have given birth to a healthy baby just ten months before?"

Michael wondered if it could be that simple, if a crime lord could be fooled that easily. "What about you? Does this mobster blame you for helping Beverly and Reed?"

She shook her head. "No. I took Beverly home, returning her to her family. They didn't hold me accountable. But they made it clear that they'd never forgive my brother. He was part of their organization.

He understood the consequences of his actions. He was warned to stay away from Beverly, and now that she's sick, they blame him for not taking care of her. For all those months she didn't receive medical treatment.''

Michael cursed beneath his breath. Trust Reed to get caught up in the mob, to fall for the boss's daughter, to lure Heather into a web of deceit and danger.

"Who does the mob think Justin's father is?" he asked, although he already knew. Heaven help him, he knew.

"You," she said.

Yes, him. Who else could it be? He was Heather's only lover, the only man she'd ever given herself to. And he was dark-skinned and dark-eyed, just like the baby.

He gazed at Heather, at her blond hair and fair complexion, at the sleek, simple clothes hugging her curves.

In the old days, she had been his best friend's little sister, a sweet, skinny kid with big blue eyes, tagging along like a homeless filly.

Then she'd begun to mature. By the time she was sixteen, she'd blossomed into a lean, leggy beauty, an obsession eighteen-year-old Michael could barely control.

But as willing as she'd been, he hadn't touched her. He'd promised Reed that he wouldn't.

Michael could still recall the day Heather had confronted him, the sunny afternoon she'd challenged that promise.

They'd been at the edge of the lake, skimming stones across the water. She'd been wearing shorts and a halter top, her hair shimmering in glorious waves.

"Why haven't you ever kissed me?" she'd asked.

He'd dropped the stone in his hand, plunking it in the water.

"You're still a kid," he told her.

"No, I'm not." She came toward him, as fresh as the Hill Country air, as graceful as a palomino. "I'm all grown up."

Blood rushed from his head to his feet. She was everything he wanted. And more. "You're jailbait."

She frowned, and he could see that he'd wounded her. He knew she had feelings for him, an attraction that had deepened over the years.

But she was dangerous. He spent too many nights thinking about her. Fantasizing. Driving himself crazy with what he longed to do to her. "You're Reed's sister. I promised him I'd stay away."

"You and Reed hardly get along anymore."

"It doesn't matter. It was still a promise. I can't go back on my word." He shoved his hands in his pockets, doing his damnedest not to touch her, to hold her, to feel her heartbeat stumble against his. "Come see me when you're eighteen." When her brother couldn't interfere. "Ask me to kiss you then."

Instead she'd asked him to marry her, right then and there, in a secret Cherokee ceremony. Then they could be together, she'd said, no matter how old she was.

For an instant, one torturous instant, Michael had been tempted. Just to be with her, just to take what she was offering.

In the end, he'd told her it was a crazy idea. But so was trying to get her out of his system.

He'd spent the next two years, the next twenty-four months dating other girls, other blondes who never quite filled the ache—the desperate, sexual consumption.

Then finally, on Heather's eighteenth birthday, she'd come to him. Without the slightest hesitation, he'd made love to her, taking her virginity, making her his.

Yet no matter how many times they joined, how many hot, torrid nights they climaxed in each other's arms, he feared the obsession, the emotional power she wielded over him.

Michael didn't want to fall in love. He'd seen how it had affected his mother, the destruction it caused. The only man she'd ever loved, Michael's freewheeling father, had kicked her square in the heart.

The way Heather had eventually done to him.

He should have never asked her to live with him. He—

"Michael?"

He cleared his mind. Or tried to. The past still seemed like the present—the frustration, the emotional turmoil, the fear. "What?"

"I need your help."

He squinted. "With what?"

"With the baby."

He glanced at Justin. The kid tested the perimeters of his confinement, holding on to the sides and rattling the cage. "How so?"

"I need you to commit to being his father."

Michael's pulse shot up his arm. "You said the West Coast family already thinks I am."

"I know, but everyone else has to think that, too.

If we don't keep up the pretense they might find out the truth.''

"You have no right to ask this of me. To expect me to raise your brother's son.''

"I'm not expecting you to do it forever. Just for a few months.''

He almost glanced at Justin again, then decided not to. What if the boy flashed one of those big, goofy grins? Smiled at him the way he'd smiled at Heather?

She set her coffee aside, and he suspected it had gone cold. As cold as the blood flowing through his veins. He didn't want to play papa to Reed Black-wood's baby, not even for a short time.

"I've worked out the details,'' she told him. "I'll stay in Texas for a few months, and we can feign a reunion. But our attempt to renew our relationship will fail, and I'll leave town to start a new life. For appearance's sake, we'll keep in touch about the baby. You'll be the concerned father without having to get too involved.''

He gave her an incredulous look. Did she think that feigning a relationship wasn't getting involved? Or publicly claiming a child who wasn't his?

"What makes you think I don't have a new woman in my life, that I'm not dating someone?'' he asked, reminding her of how long she'd been gone.

Her voice quavered. "Do you? Are you?''

"No.'' But he was glad to see the suggestion had rattled her, that he'd planted a seed to make her wonder. The way he'd wondered for eighteen grueling months if she'd run off with another man, if that had been the reason she'd disappeared.

"You should have risked a phone call, Heather. You should have called me. Just once.''

"I wanted to. So many times, I wanted to."

"But you didn't."

She glanced at the mist-fogged window, at the overcast light shadowing the room. "I thought about you every day."

He'd thought about her, too. She was always there, the beautiful ghost from his past, the girl who'd disappeared.

She twisted her hands on her lap, and he noticed her nails were bitten to the quick. He considered apologizing for the barb about another woman, but decided he would sound like a wuss, like he was still obsessed with her.

He held his ground. "Why didn't you think about me before you took off to California? Before you got tangled up in this mess?"

"You wouldn't allow me to see my own brother. What was I supposed to do?"

Michael turned cynical. "Everything is always about Reed."

"This is about Justin. An innocent child." Her eyes turned watery. "Please understand. This is important. More important than you can imagine. Beverly's dad will probably keep an eye on us, just to see if we hear from Reed. He'll probably try to lure information from people we know. So I need to make sure everyone we socialize with believes Justin is our baby. If a rumor leaks that he could be Reed's son—"

He cursed before she could finish her sentence. What in the hell was he supposed to do? Ignore her plea? Let the mob take the boy away from her?

"Two months," he said. "And I'm explaining the entire farce to my uncle."

"No!" She nearly flew off the sofa. "You can't

tell anyone. Not another living soul. This has to be our secret. The lie we take to our graves.''

''It isn't right.'' He hadn't lied to his uncle since he was a kid, a smart-mouthed youth who hadn't given a damn about anyone but himself.

''Please.'' She went to the baby and picked him up. ''Please.''

Michael frowned, and Justin took that moment to smile, to blow bubbles at him.

Damn. Damn. Damn.

''All right,'' he said as the boy's slobbery grin tunneled an unwelcome path straight to his cautious, it'll-be-over-in-two-months heart.

The day passed quickly, but as evening rolled around, Heather grew more and more anxious.

Michael had gone to work that morning and that was the last she'd seen of him.

She'd kept busy, baby-proofing the house the best she could, moving Justin's crib, unloading her rental car, preparing the guest room for Justin and herself.

She'd cleaned everything. She'd even dusted the third bedroom, the one filled with junk Michael had been storing for years.

And like Suzy-homemaker, she'd organized the kitchen cupboards, too.

Then she'd gotten the brilliant idea to fix dinner, believing quite foolishly that Michael would come home in time to eat.

The table was set and the food had gone cold. It wasn't a fancy meal, considering the simple contents in Michael's fridge, but she made a pretty good meat loaf. And he liked mashed potatoes, with pools of melting butter instead of gravy.

She sat at the table and fidgeted with a bowl of wilting green beans. She'd lost her appetite hours ago. Deciding to clean up, she headed to the kitchen for aluminum foil and plastic containers.

What was she doing? Trying to resume where they left off? If he hadn't loved her then, what made her think he would fall in love with her now? That the next two months would change her life?

She needed Michael to help her set the stage, to establish Justin's paternity, but beyond that, she had no right to expect anything more.

Want it, crave it, but not expect it.

She wrapped the meat loaf and scooped the potatoes into a plastic bowl, closing the vacuum-sealed lid. Then the front door rattled, and her heartbeat tripled.

Michael was home.

Should she greet him? Or continue clearing the table? Cursing her quaking hands, she chose the table. How could a man she'd known for over half her life make her so nervous?

Because she'd loved him for over half her life, and he'd always given her butterflies.

She heard him moving around in the living room. Removing his hat, most likely, brushing the moisture from his clothes.

She pictured him, as he was, tall and dark, amid the homespun furnishings. Michael had inherited the old farmhouse from his mother, a hardworking waitress who'd acquired it from her ancestors—German immigrants who'd settled in the Texas Hill Country.

The house bore hardwood floors, paned windows and hand-stenciled trim that dressed up door frames and plain walls. A live oak in the front yard stood guard throughout the year, and bluebonnets blanketed the ground every spring.

As Heather made a face at the green beans, wondering if she should toss them out, Michael entered the dining room.

"You made dinner?"

She looked up. His hair was long and loose and slightly damp. "Yes." She wished she'd thought to remove the two place settings, the scented candle still burning. The romantic ambience, she thought. "Are you hungry? It's cold, but I can reheat it."

"I grabbed a bite in town."

"Oh." She fidgeted with a fan-shaped napkin, suddenly embarrassed that she'd folded it that way. "So you went out?"

"Yeah. Did you think I was working all this time?"

She shrugged as if his whereabouts didn't matter. Then she couldn't stop herself from asking. "Where'd you go?"

He shifted his stance. "To have a few beers."

"At the Corral?"

"Yes."

So he'd gone to the local honky-tonk. "What'd you do there?"

"I just told you. I had a few beers."

He didn't play pool? Or dance? Or flirt with the country barflies? The bimbos with their big hairdos and tight jeans? "So that's all you did?"

He peered in the foil-wrapped package, checking out the meat loaf. "Yep. That's all."

"I cleaned the house," she said, changing the subject, hating herself for feeling like a suspicious lover.

"You didn't have to. I don't expect you to pick up after me. I never did."

"I needed to baby-proof the place."

"Oh." He broke off a corner of the meat loaf, ate it, then caught himself. "I guess I worked up another appetite."

Doing what? she wondered. "I'll fix you a plate."

"This is fine." He took a few slices and devoured them cold. Next he uncapped the mashed potatoes and ate a large portion directly from the bowl.

Hardly the intimate meal she'd planned. "Did you tell anyone about me and Justin?"

He tasted the soggy green beans. "No."

"Not even Bobby?"

"My uncle was busy today."

"Too busy to talk to you?"

Now it was Michael's turn to shrug. "I didn't feel like going into all of it."

An ache, as solid as the hills, slammed into her heart. He hadn't felt like talking about her, the woman he'd lived with, the woman who still loved him. "Seems to me that a man whose girlfriend just returned to him with his baby would've explained the situation to his family instead of going out for a few beers."

He raised his brows, two wicked slashes of black over exotic-shaped eyes. "Justin isn't my son."

"He's supposed to be, Michael."

"But he isn't."

She wanted to cry, to sink to the floor and weep. The way she'd cried over the other pony. "You can't act this way, not if we're going to tell people that Justin is our baby."

"Then give me a day or so to get used to it. To cope with the idea."

"Fine." She carried the dishes into the kitchen, going back and forth, putting away the leftovers.

"Where is the kid?"

"Asleep. It's after ten. Or hadn't you noticed?"

"You're not my girlfriend anymore, Heather. I don't have to stay home at night."

Her chest hurt again, with pain and fury, heartbreak and devastation. "Yes, you do. We're supposed to be reconciling."

His eyes blazed. "Does that mean I get to sleep with you? Get my hot-and-nasty fill before I kick you out?"

Heather froze. Was that the way he thought of her, of the nights they'd spent in each other's arms?

She wanted to throw a plate at him, but she'd already cleared the table. "Not on your life, buster. And when the time comes, I'll be leaving on my own."

"Of course you will. You already left once. How hard can it be to walk out a second time?"

She banked her fury. She *was* the one who'd taken off, who'd lied about why she'd gone to California. "I never meant to stay away."

"But you did. And now you're back with Reed's son."

"Our son, Michael. You have to start thinking of him as our son."

The edge in his voice softened, but his stance remained defensive. "Was Reed okay about you bringing Justin to me? About me pretending to be his father?"

"Yes. He thinks you'll make a good dad. That you'll treat Justin right." But Reed also thought that

Michael loved her, that he'd loved her for years. Of course she doubted that Michael would believe that Reed had interceded for him, giving their relationship his blessing. "He doesn't hate you the way you hate him."

"Yes, he does. He's just telling you what you want to hear. He's always done that."

Telling her what she wanted to hear—like Michael loving her. "He's my brother. It's his job to protect me."

"The way he protected you from getting caught up in the mob?"

Weary, Heather closed her eyes. "I don't want to talk about Reed." To think about him running for the rest of his life, mourning his wife and son.

When she opened her eyes, Michael was staring, watching her eyelids flutter. Self-conscious, she took a deep breath. He used to watch her sleep, and then wake her with a stirring kiss.

"I'm sorry," he said. "I know you've been through a rough time."

"Yes." And losing him was making everything that much harder.

He reached out as if to smooth a strand of her hair away from her face, but drew back and shoved his hands into his pockets. "I should get to bed."

She let out the breath she'd been holding. "Me, too."

A few seconds later, their gazes locked, making the moment even more awkward.

She broke eye contact first, blowing out the candle, sending the flame dancing before it disappeared.

Then she and Michael separated, and like the wounded ex-lovers they'd become, they drifted into different bedrooms.

And closed their doors without making a sound.

Three

Michael heard the shower running and the baby crying.

Great. He buttoned his shirt and tucked it into his jeans. Another anxiety-ridden morning.

Should he let Justin cry? Ignore the baby's angry wails and let Heather deal with him after she finished her shower?

Yeah, he thought. That was exactly what he should do. Yet as he reached for his boots, the kid's bawling made him guilty.

What if the little guy was sick? Or afraid? Or—

Oh, hell.

Michael shoved on his boots. Heather could be in the shower forever. Washing that hair of hers was a major task. He knew. He'd shampooed it for her plenty of times. And like the idiot he was, he still had fantasies about her hair—the way it streamed down her back, slid through his fingers when he kissed her.

Which, he warned himself, was something he shouldn't be thinking about.

Justin let out another wail, and Michael gave up and went into the kid's room.

The baby stood in his portable crib, screaming like a pint-sized banshee. When he spotted Michael, he gulped, and then cried some more.

"What's the matter?" Michael asked.

The boy gulped again. Tears streamed down his face, and his hair, tousled from sleep, stuck out at odd angles. He had thick, dark hair. A lot like Reed's. Or mine, Michael thought.

Justin made a distressed face. "Pa...pa...pa."

Papa? Daddy? Was he crying for Reed?

"I can't help you, buddy. I have no idea where your papa is."

The boy glanced at the floor. "Pa."

Michael looked down, then saw the stuffed animal at his feet. "Is this what all the commotion is about?" He reached for the toy, a yellow horse with threads of gold in its mane. "Here." He handed it over, and the kid snatched it like candy.

Justin hiccupped and hugged the horse, and Michael ruffled the boy's messy hair. "Let's see if I can find something to dry your eyes."

He looked around the room and noticed a bunch of baby junk on the dresser. Diapers, pop-up wipes, lotion. He studied the wipes. Would it be all right to clean the kid's face with disposable cloths designed to wipe his bottom? Like the packets of wet-napkins barbecue joints handed out? Or the fancy ones the chef at the ranch provided?

Unsure of what else to do, Michael untucked his shirt and used the end of it, dabbing the child's face. He wasn't sure if butt wipes had the same ingredients as face wipes, and he wasn't about to make a stupid mistake and irritate the boy's eyes.

"There. That's better."

Justin rewarded him with a goofy grin.

"I guess you think so, too."

"Pa." The kid held out his horse.

Michael took the toy, wondering what the hell he was supposed to do with it. Then he spotted the key on the side. "Does it talk?" He wound the key and a lullaby played. "Oh, I see. It's a musical horse. Can't say I'm familiar with the tune, though."

He handed the stuffed animal back to Justin, and the boy shot him another one of those goofy grins. Well, what do you know? He had dimples, kind of like Shirley Temple. Or Baby Face Nelson. After all, this was Reed's kid.

Justin blew bubbles, and Michael wondered what Heather intended to tell the boy when he was older. The truth, of course. She couldn't let Justin grow up not knowing his true parentage.

Could she?

"I'm only going to be your dad for a few months. So don't get used to this."

The kid handed over the horse again.

"All right, fine. We'll play the song one more time."

Just as Michael turned the key, the door opened.

Damn. There stood Heather in a bathrobe, her damp hair teasing the terry cloth.

"Justin was throwing a fit," he said. "He dropped his horse."

She tilted her head. He wasn't close enough to inhale her fragrance, but he knew she favored fruit-scented soaps and shampoos.

"Pony."

The robe gapped, just a bit. She wasn't wearing a bra. That much he could tell. But whether she'd donned a pair of panties was anybody's guess. "What?"

"It's a pony."

"Pa," Justin parroted.

Michael glanced at the toy in his hand. Pa meant pony?

"Oh. Okay." Feeling foolish, he gave Justin his furry companion. The dang thing plunked out a song while Heather's robe played a distracting game of peekaboo.

Why would she be wearing panties? She'd just climbed out of the shower.

"I'll show you how to change a diaper," she said.

He took a step back. Making the transition from her half-naked body to diapering a baby didn't register, not in his befuddled mind. "What for?"

"Because you're supposed to be learning to be a dad."

There she went, trying to get him into the Daddy mode, to embellish his short-lived role. "You can show me, but I'm not going to do it, especially if he's stinky."

"He's wet."

"How can you tell?"

"Because he's wet every morning."

She placed Justin on the bed and unsnapped his pajamas. Once he was exposed, she covered him, much too quickly, then reached for the wipes.

Michael rolled his eyes. Was she worried about the baby's modesty? "I've seen one of those before, Heather. In fact, I think I have one." He glanced at his fly. "Yep, sure enough, I do."

She rolled her eyes right back at him. "Little boys tend to spray."

"Really?" He couldn't help but chuckle. "Has he ever got you?"

"No, but he got Reed."

"Oh, yeah?" He poked the baby's belly. "So you peed on your dad, huh? I'll bet that put Mr. Hardened Criminal in his place."

Justin laughed, and Michael grinned. "My sentiments exactly."

Heather shook her head. "That's not funny."

"Then why are you cracking a smile?"

"I'm not." But she was, and they both knew it. She'd always had a silly sense of humor, even where her hard-ass brother was concerned.

While Justin squirmed and kicked his feet, she utilized the baby supplies on the dresser, wiping him down and protecting his skin with lotion.

Afterward, she put him on the floor and let him crawl, and the kid scooted through the bedroom like a windup toy.

"Thanks for watching him while I was in the shower."

"I just picked up his pony." But in the future, Michael wasn't going to cater to the little tyke. As cute as Justin was, he wasn't up for spoiling Reed's kid. Nor did he intend to spend his mornings making light-hearted conversation with Heather.

Her robe was gaping again, and the walls were

closing in. ''I better go. I've got a full day ahead.''
He still had to tell his uncle that Heather was back.

And lie about Justin being their son.

Michael caught up with his uncle at the office in
the barn. Bobby Elk divided his time between giving
riding lessons in the arena and hosting guided tours
in the hills. Of course, these days, the wealthy rancher
was content to stay home with his wife and baby son.

He'd earned his right to happiness, Michael
thought. Bobby had lost his first wife in an auto accident, a crash that had also left him an amputee. But
that didn't slow him down. He wore a prosthetic limb
and was as active and athletic as any cowboy Michael
knew.

''Hey,'' Bobby said, glancing up from his desk. His
workspace, as usual, was spotless.

The desk on the other side of the room, the one
assigned to Michael, was cluttered with folders, files
and candy wrappers. But so was his primary office at
the lodge. He preferred a bit of disorder. It was his
rebellion, his supposed. His way of not quite con-
forming.

Other than that, he was pretty damn responsible.
Okay, so maybe he was notoriously late for meetings.
And on long, dark, lonely nights, he watched dirty
movies and got drunker than a celibate skunk. But at
least he hadn't turned out like Reed.

Michael removed his hat and tossed it on his desk.
Bobby's Stetson shielded his eyes, and his hair was
plaited into its customary braid.

He'd taught Michael and Reed about being Cherokee, but neither had welcomed the older man's spir-
itual teachings. They'd thought it was Indian bull, a

bunch of warrior crap. Both had been sired by Cherokee cowboys who hadn't given a damn about them, and their resentment ran deep.

But little by little, Bobby's lessons had begun to penetrate their thick skulls. Even Reed started following the red road, for all the good it had done.

"Do you have a minute?" Michael asked.

Bobby glanced up again. "Sure. What's on your mind?"

"Heather's back."

His uncle's expression froze. "She's home?"

"Yep." Home.

"And?" Bobby came around and sat on the edge of his desk.

"She...we..." How in the hell was he going to lie to his uncle, the man who'd taken care of Michael's dying mother, built this ranch, treated him like a son?

"What's wrong? Where has she been?"

"With Reed. They..." He stalled, unsure how much he was allowed to reveal. He should have asked Heather. He should have—

"Michael," Bobby pressed.

"Reed was hiding out from some criminals, and Heather was with him. She wasn't able to come back until now."

"Is Reed all right?"

"As far as I know." Eliminating the Mafia details, he continued, "The main thing I wanted to tell you is that Heather had a baby while she was gone. My baby."

There. He'd done it. He'd spouted the lie, said it with as much conviction as he could muster.

"Wow." Stunned, Bobby could only stare. "A boy or a girl?"

"A boy. He's ten months old, and his name is Justin."

"That's incredible."

"Yeah."

For a moment, they both fell silent, then his uncle said, "Are you okay with all of this? It's got to be a shock. And I know how uncomfortable you are about—"

"Illegitimacy?" Michael provided, before Bobby could finish. He knew damn well that would cross his uncle's mind. Michael had sworn long ago that he would never impregnate a woman without marrying her. That he wouldn't do what his dad had done.

But now Heather had put him in a position to defend himself. "Heather and I are trying to work things out, but it's a little tense right now."

"I understand."

Michael nodded. Bobby's child had been conceived out of wedlock, and at the time, he hadn't intended to marry his pregnant lover. Of course, this situation was different; it wasn't even real. "Do you think you could spread the word? Let folks know Heather is back. And mention Justin. I don't want to have to tell everyone myself." He paused to take a much-needed breath. "And I'd appreciate it if you'd ask them to give Heather and I some space. I'm not ready to have people stopping by with cakes or pies or anything."

"No problem. I'll take care of it."

"Thanks. I'm going to take off. I've got some things to do at the lodge."

Bobby reached around for the coffee on his desk. "Will you let me know when I can see your son? And Heather?"

Michael nodded, and then grabbed his hat and

ducked out the door, dreading the deception he'd already begun to live.

Heather didn't know what to do. The big dog continued to scratch and bark at the door. He even howled a few times, a war cry that would wake the dead.

Or a sleeping baby who'd fussed before his nap.

Heather made a face. Now the dog had taken to yapping, and his choppy, high-pitched barks pierced her eardrums.

She'd gotten a good look at him through the screen door and had locked herself in. He was the ugliest, mangiest beast she'd ever seen. He probably had fleas and ticks and Lord knew what else.

Rabies?

That does it. It was time to call Michael. She still remembered his cell phone number.

While the dog yapped and whined and attempted to claw his way into the house, she punched out the digits.

Cell phones were a security hazard, with or without a bug. But did it matter? The mob wouldn't care about this call. It rang several times, and she prayed Michael's voice mail didn't pick up. Tracking him down at the ranch would be next to impossible. The man never kept a schedule.

"H'lo?"

"Michael, it's Heather."

The line went silent, and she cursed his wariness. You'd think she had a mouth-foaming disease. Speaking of which…

"There's this huge creature at the door, and he

won't go away. He's barking and howling and scratching—"

"That's Chester."

"What?"

"Chester. My dog."

That ratty, flea-bitten canine was his pet?

"How does he look?" Michael asked.

Was he kidding? "Like the hound from hell."

A chuckle came across the line. "Yep. That's Chester all right. He's been out carousing. He always does that. Then after a few days, he drags his sorry ass home looking for a warm bed and a tasty meal."

"You let that beast run wild? Mate with other dogs?"

"Naw. He's fixed. He just thinks his equipment is still intact."

Heather twisted the phone cord, wrapping it around her wrist. "He better not be a leg humper."

Michael had the gall to laugh. "I've never seen him do that. Of course, he did stick his nose up this hot chick's dress."

She glared at the phone. What hot chick?

"He only did it once, though."

"Once is enough."

"Yeah, but you can't blame a guy for trying."

Wanna bet? "Just what am I supposed to do? I'm locked in the house with a napping baby, and your loyal pet is trying to dig a hole through the front door."

"So let him in. He won't hurt you."

"You can't be serious. He's big and ugly. And filthy," she added.

"He must have been playing in the mud. Running

around in the rain and all. Hold tight, I'll come by to clean him up.''

Hold tight? While the dog tunneled his way into the house? "You better get here soon.''

"I will.''

They hung up, and she waited.

Then waited some more.

The baby woke with a wailing cry, so she picked him up and brought him into the living room to wait with her. His sleepy eyes grew wide and bright. When he waved his hands, flailing them in front of her face, she tried to settle him down.

"It's just Daddy's dog, honey.''

"Da…da…da…da.''

"Yes. Daddy's dog.'' Cujo, she thought.

Finally she heard Michael's truck, and after she was certain he'd gotten the hound under control, she opened the door and peered through the screen.

Justin made an excited sound, and she balanced him on her hip.

In the front yard, Michael was attempting to bathe the creature. As he lathered and hosed and cursed his way through it, Justin laughed.

Heather laughed, too. Finally Cujo, or Chester, or whatever his name was, shook his big, black body and sprayed his master with water.

Justin clapped, and Michael and the dog appeared at the screen door.

"Who gave who a bath?'' Heather asked.

"Very funny. Will you grab me some towels?''

She left and returned with a small stack. Opening the screen a smidgen, she slid them through the narrow space. He dried himself first, then went after the dog.

"Come on out and meet him," Michael said.

Heather hugged the baby. "What if he tries to bite Justin?"

"He likes kids."

"He'd better."

"He does. I swear."

"Fine." She crept outside and held fast to her son, the baby she'd vowed to protect.

Justin flapped his arms, and she hoped the strange dog didn't mistake him for a bird. The beast wiggled and whined.

Michael guided Heather and Justin to the porch swing, and the dog followed.

"Chester, say hello to Heather."

The dog plopped his butt down and stuck out his paw.

"Oh, my." She hadn't expected such manners. She shook his paw, and Justin squealed in baby delight.

"Da...da...da...da."

"You want to meet the doggy?" Michael asked. "Come on." He placed a dry towel on his lap and took the boy from Heather.

He let Justin pat the pooch, and the dog nuzzled the child's hand.

"Oh, my," Heather said again. Chester was as gentle as a lamb. An ugly lamb, with a pointed snout, droopy eyes and enormous ears. "Where'd you get him, Michael?"

"At the pound. I was...it was..." He paused and cleared his throat. "I got him a few months after you left. I needed somebody to keep me company. The house was so damn quiet, and Chester livened up the place."

"Oh." Guilty, she watched the dog drop his head

onto Michael's knee. Justin leaned forward, anxious to pet Chester again.

"See, they like each other."

"Yes." She blinked, hoping she wouldn't cry. Michael looked so right with an adoring baby on his lap and a loyal dog at his feet.

He rocked the swing, and Justin snuggled against his chest. Chester settled down to let his damp fur dry.

"It's nice out," Michael said.

She nodded. The afternoon air was warm and the flowers were rich and blue. "It's always pretty after a storm. After the rain nourishes the ground."

Justin closed his eyes and began to drift off, but he hadn't finished his nap earlier.

"Did you get your clothes out of my room, Heather?"

"No. Not yet." She'd seen them in his closet when she'd swept for bugs. "But I will." She was surprised that he hadn't given them to charity. Or burned them.

"Your old lingerie drawer has some stuff in it, too."

"I know. I saw them. Is my car still in the garage?"

"Yes. But the battery's dead."

"I have to return the rental by Friday," she said. "I can't afford to keep it."

"I'll make sure your car gets a new battery. That it's running right again."

"Thank you," she whispered. "I appreciate all of your help."

Their eyes met, and her stomach fluttered with girlish little wings. In the silence, she watched as he stroked Justin's back, soothing the baby with a gentle motion, lulling him into a deeper sleep.

A moment later, he stopped rocking the swing and stilled his hand, as though suddenly aware of the tenderness, of the family setting.

Man, woman, child, dog.

"I need to go back to work."

He handed Justin to her, and she took the boy with a heavy heart. The child stirred and went back to sleep.

"You can deal with Chester now, can't you?"

"Yes." She glanced at the dog, and he looked up and perked his big, floppy ears. "What should I feed him?"

"Anything. He eats table scraps."

"I'll give him some leftovers for now, then offer him whatever I fix later. Maybe chicken. I noticed some drumsticks in the freezer."

"That's fine, but don't count on me for dinner. I'll probably be late again tonight." Michael rose and dusted his jeans, leaving the dry towel on the swing. "Don't wait up."

"I won't," she said, even though she knew she would lie in bed and think about him.

The man who didn't want to stay home.

Four

Heather couldn't sleep. She'd tried to, but her mind wouldn't shut down. She couldn't stop thinking about Beverly and Reed, about Michael and herself.

She missed Reed and Beverly, but somehow she missed Michael even more. Missed being his partner, his lover, his friend.

She sat on the couch in the living room, a low lamp burning, and drew her knees up. Chester snuggled beside her. He was half asleep, his droopy eyes sagging even more.

"You're such a good dog." She rubbed his ears, and he scooted closer and put his head on her lap.

"Are you lonely?" His master wasn't home yet, and the DVD clock read 1:04 in bright red numbers.

"You sleep in Michael's bed, don't you?" She stroked his thick, coarse fur. "I used to sleep there."

And she missed every moment of being near him, of waking in his arms.

Another digit turned on the clock, then another. Time passed in slow motion. She remained on the sofa, her legs curled beneath her.

Then she heard Michael's truck. Chester perked his ears, and Heather's heartbeat slammed against her chest. Should she feign sleep? He'd told her not to wait up, yet here she was, waiting up.

Not purposely, but she was up just the same.

A key rattled in the doorknob.

Too late to feign sleep. The dog thumped his tail, then whined.

Michael entered the house and spotted her and Chester immediately. The dog jumped off the sofa to greet his master, and Heather smoothed her nightgown.

Nerves jangled in her stomach, and an ocean pounded in her ears. Why did he always affect her that way? Why couldn't she stay calm at the sight of him?

Michael bent to return Chester's affection, but his eyes were on Heather. "I didn't expect to see you," he said.

"I couldn't sleep, and I didn't want to disturb the baby."

He rose to his full height and sent her hormones tripping and stumbling.

She recalled every inch of his body: wide shoulders, sculpted muscles, lean hips. On his right biceps, he sported an armband tattoo, a tribal design inked in bold, black shapes.

As a girl, Heather had been fascinated by his rebellious sexuality. As a woman, he'd never failed to leave her breathless.

"I went to the Corral again," he said.

"I know."

"How do you know?"

"I can tell." She met his gaze, saw the waning, self-medicated look in his eyes. "You've been drinking."

"I'm not drunk."

She knew that, too. He didn't drive drunk.

He leaned against the entertainment center. "I don't know what to do with myself. This is so damn hard."

She tore at her damaged nails. "I'm sorry I caused you so much trouble."

"I'll get over it."

Would he? She wasn't sure.

But she'd never been sure about Michael. He could smile one minute and turn surly the next. Sometimes he was her best friend, and other times he seemed like a stranger. He kept corners of himself hidden: deep, dark places he wouldn't allow anyone to touch.

She'd tried to light those corners, to slip into his soul the way he'd penetrated hers, but she'd fallen short.

Michael tossed his keys onto a shelf. "I wonder where he is. Do you know where he is?"

She knew he meant Reed. Odd that he should be thinking about her brother now. Reed and Michael were cut from the same rough, ragged cloth, with a love-hate relationship she'd never been able to grasp. "No, I don't. But I expect to hear from him."

He started. "How? When?"

"We agreed to a phone call. We have a specific

date set aside. Near the end of the month.'' Reed needed to know that his son was safe, that the child he'd given up was healthy and happy.

Michael's voice turned bitter. ''A phone call? He's going to call you, but you couldn't contact me all those months?''

She tried not to flinch, to react to his tone, to the chill in his eyes. ''This is different. It'll be on a secure line.''

''From where?''

''Here.'' She motioned to the desk, where the phone rested. ''Reed gave me a scrambler like one he'll use. With a unit at the end of each telephone, our call will be encrypted.''

''So it won't matter if the phones are bugged?''

''No, but I'd feel safer knowing the lines are clear before he calls. If the equipment malfunctioned, if we were found out...'' She let her words fade, disappear into the stillness of the room.

''Where was he the last time you saw him?''

''Does it matter?'' She watched Michael take off his jacket, toss it carelessly over a chair. ''He's moved on by now.''

''Good riddance, I say.''

How could he be so cold? So callous? ''I wish you didn't hate Reed so much.''

''And I wish you'd stop defending him.''

''I can't.'' Not after the grief they'd shared, the tears they'd cried. What they'd suffered as adults was far worse than the turmoil from their childhood. ''He's the only family I have left. He and Justin.''

''He screwed with our lives, Heather.''

''Why? Because he kept us apart when I was younger?''

"First I wasn't permitted to touch you. And later he tried to muscle me into marrying you. He tried to dictate every aspect of our relationship. Every single thing that happened between us."

"He did?" She hadn't been privy to Michael and Reed's arguments, to the shoving matches they'd refused to discuss.

How could her brother humiliate her like that? And why did he claim that Michael was in love with her? What did he base that opinion on?

Tired of being hurt, she cursed both men. "He was wrong, but so were you."

"Me?"

"Yes, you." At least Reed cared. At least he was looking out for her. "You had no right to ban me from my brother. In spite of his brutish methods, he meant well."

"He was interfering in our lives."

"By hoping you'd marry me?"

Michael merely looked at her, but she could see that she'd struck a nerve.

"It was more than that."

"Was it?" she challenged, stung by the thought. She'd always suspected that he didn't want to marry her, that he scoffed at the notion of happily-ever-after, but to see it on his face erupted like a sudden slap across the cheek.

"Your brother is an ex-con. A thief."

"He's a good man, misguided but good. And you turned your back on him."

"Oh, yeah?" He moved closer. "You call claiming his son turning my back on him? I agreed to be that little boy's father. To tell everyone he's mine."

She blinked, stunned by the emotion in his voice.

By the sheer impact of what he was saying. The child Reed had entrusted to him was a responsibility he couldn't deny, a gesture of Cherokee brotherhood.

He jammed his hands into his pockets, and she felt her eyes water. She couldn't help but think about the other pony.

The other baby.

She'd gone to California carrying Michael's child, yet she could never tell him, never admit what had happened to their son.

She'd had her reasons for leaving town without telling him she was pregnant. Reasons that hurt now as much as the day she'd boarded that L.A.-bound plane.

Michael turned toward the window. "It's creepy."

She followed his gaze. What did he see? Mist-covered flowers? A moonlit sky? Shadowed hills?

In her mind's eye, she saw a grave. A leather-wrapped bundle in a little wooden box.

"What do you mean?" she asked.

"This whole thing with the mob. It's like the night has eyes."

"No one is out there."

"How can you be sure?"

"I can't," she admitted.

He shifted to look at her. "How did you live like this for a year and a half? How did you stand it?"

"I didn't have a choice." She thought about their baby again, the tiny being she'd cradled in her womb.

He dragged a hand through his hair. "I wish things would have turned out differently."

"Me, too," she whispered as he glanced away, leaving her alone with her memories. And a regretful heart.

* * *

Three days later, Michael swore beneath his breath. Heather fixed her makeup, and he scraped a razor across his jaw.

Did she have to look so damn good? So lean? So leggy?

Her time in the bathroom was supposed to be up, but she'd dashed back in, claiming she would only be a minute, that her mascara had smeared.

They used to share confined spaces without a hitch, but things had been different then. They'd been lovers.

"I'm looking forward to meeting Bobby's wife," she said, swiping a cotton swab below her eye.

Michael didn't respond. They were getting ready for a dinner engagement at his uncle's house. Their first public appearance, so to speak, as a reconciling couple, as parents of a ten-month-old baby.

He'd agreed to this farce, and now he was stuck playing his part. How was he supposed to behave? Would his discomfort show? His confusion? His hunger for a woman who'd hurt him?

He finished shaving and turned to look at her. Her hair streamed like a waterfall, and her blouse revealed a hint of cleavage. A skirt flared at her hips and a wide leather belt cinched her waist.

And her face. Those bright blue eyes. That full, lush mouth.

"How in the hell are we going to pull this off?" he asked.

"You mean tonight?"

"We'll probably be tense around each other the entire time. We're in over our heads."

Silent, Heather glanced at her nails. She'd filed and

painted them, but they still seemed ragged, Michael thought. Chewed to the bone.

Obviously she was nervous, too. As worried as he was.

"Maybe we should kiss," she said.

His pulse skyrocketed. "What?"

Her voice turned quiet, almost shy. "To let off a little steam. To get used to each other again."

He wanted to yell at her, to tell her she was crazy. The last thing they should do was taste what they'd been missing. But as she wet her lips, a hot, syrupy shiver slid up his spine.

"Do really think it will work?" he asked stupidly.

"We could try."

Yeah, try. At this point, he was willing to do almost anything to curb his appetite for her.

"Just this once," he said.

She moistened her lips again. "Okay."

He took a rough breath, and their gazes locked. Suddenly their reflections shimmered in the mirror. Her delicate profile. The glint of his belt buckle. The fluid line of her hair.

They used to make naughty jokes about putting mirrors on the ceiling. Making reckless love and watching each other.

Heaven help me, he thought. I shouldn't be doing this.

But he did it anyway. He leaned into her, inhaling her fragrance, the sweet scent of her skin.

She leaned forward, too. He made an unintelligible sound and their mouths came together, as haunting as a memory, as forbidden as a fantasy.

He wanted to put his hands all over her, but he held back, afraid he would go too far.

She touched him instead. Tunneling her fingers through his hair, she tugged his mouth deeper to hers.

His mind fogged, like a danger-sought dream, like mist on a warm, wicked night. When his heart gripped his chest, he knew being this close to her was a mistake.

Michael pulled back. Their tongues had barely mated, and their bodies had barely brushed.

But he could still taste her.

He glanced at their reflections, wishing he wasn't left with wishes and wants and sexual mysteries of things they'd never done.

He caught her gaze in the mirror, and her breath rushed out.

He noticed her nipples were hard. But she had sensitive nipples. She stimulated easily.

Just like him.

"I have to finish getting ready," he told her, waving her off, sending her away.

Wounded, Heather stepped back. "I'll go check on Justin." She turned to leave, then stopped at the door. "Michael?"

"What?"

"Did the kiss help? Even a little?"

"No," he said. It only made him want her even more, want what he shouldn't have.

And now, damn it, he couldn't help but wonder how Heather felt about him.

Did it matter?

Her fairy-tale fantasies weren't easy to live up to. He wasn't Prince Cherokee Charming. He couldn't be her everything.

So he'd evolved into a coldhearted bastard instead.

"I thought maybe...I was hoping..." Her words drifted, and she exited the room, leaving him alone.

With a pounding heart.

With the mirror.

With an image of himself he wanted to smash to smithereens.

The dinner was carefully prepared, with a buffet in the kitchen and an intimate setting in the living room, arranged for casual dining.

The decor presented Aztec prints and lodge-pole pine furnishings. Flowers, pillows and candles added touches of warmth.

Heather, Michael and Justin were the only guests, but there was enough food for second, third and fourth helpings.

Heather enjoyed an array of salads, eating an eclectic blend of vegetables and fruits. The taco fixings kept everyone busy and the guacamole thrilled Justin. He begged off Heather's plate, ignoring his bland baby meal for spoonfuls of the mildly seasoned dip.

While their infant son napped down the hall, Bobby and his wife, Julianne, exchanged outward affection. He placed his hand on her knee; she leaned her head on his shoulder.

Heather couldn't recall a time she and Michael had ever been that content.

Passionate, yes. But relaxed?

No matter how many years they'd spent together, they'd never been completely at ease. Because she was in love, and he wasn't.

"Your son is so cute," Julianne said.

Heather looked up and smiled at the other woman.

Bobby's wife was pretty and petite, with stunning red hair and a springtime complexion. "Thank you."

Michael didn't acknowledge the compliment, not until Bobby added, "The little guy looks like you, Mike."

"You think?" He shot Justin a quick glance, and the boy swallowed the avocado dip in his mouth.

"Yeah, I think." Bobby left his chair and scooped Justin up, making the child laugh.

Heather's heart turned heavy. If only Michael was that free with Justin.

"Is he this friendly with everyone?" Bobby asked.

"I'm afraid so." Heather watched the baby warm up to his new uncle. "He likes people. I know that's a good quality, but I worry about strangers." About the mob uncovering the truth, she thought.

Of course that wouldn't happen if she and Michael didn't raise any suspicions, if they fell into a natural pattern of parenthood.

"I don't think he does," Michael said.

"Does what?" Bobby made airplane noises, and Justin mimicked him.

"Look like me."

Silence hit the room, and Bobby merely stared. Heather shifted in her seat. First that humiliating kiss and now this. Michael had agreed to claim Reed's child, but he wasn't concerned about protecting that claim. About—

"He's better looking than me." Michael rose, breaking the tension. "Aren't you, buddy?"

Repairing the damage, he reached for the boy, and Justin went to him. But a few seconds later, Justin wanted to return to Bobby's arms.

Another awkward moment, Heather thought. Justin

sensed which man was more comfortable holding him.

"You've really got this daddy-thing wired." Michael stepped back, relinquishing the child to his uncle.

"Are you kidding? I was scared to death at first." Bobby kept his voice light, his tone teasing. He glanced at his wife. "Wasn't I?"

"Petrified. But mostly during the pregnancy stage."

"I missed that part." This from Michael, who turned to look at Heather.

She struggled to hold his gaze. She didn't want to think about pregnancy. About the flutter of life. The comfort of tiny kicks.

She glanced at Justin's pony. He'd brought the toy along, and now it lay on the floor, its gold-streaked mane strewn across a pillow.

The other pony was sleeping, she thought. Sleeping with the angels.

"Do you want to see the nursery?" Julianne asked.

Heather set her plate on the coffee table. "Won't it wake your baby?"

"No. He could sleep through a tornado. Of course, when he wakes up hungry, he is a tornado."

Heather smiled. It was comforting to hear another woman talk about her child. She'd held Bobby and Julianne's baby earlier in the evening, and he was as beautiful as his name—Brendan Robert Elk. Or Little Raven, as he was affectionately called. "I'd love to see the nursery."

The room was bright and cheerful, with a red-and-white crib, a sunburst pattern on the bedding and a candied-apple motif on the walls. Teddy bears occupied every corner.

The baby, who actually looked like a little raven, slept peacefully, his black hair tufted against bronzed skin.

Heather looked around. "This is wonderful. And all these bears."

"Bobby brings one home almost every week." Julianne motioned to a cluttered shelf. "I think we're running out of room."

Maybe, but the collection spoke of warmth and love, of home and hearth, of family.

A tiny gasp sounded, and Heather and Julianne turned.

Bobby entered the nursery with Justin, and the boy's eyes were as wide as saucers.

The older man balanced his young nephew. "I think someone's impressed."

"So it seems." Heather had never seen Justin so awed. But, then, he'd never been exposed to a bedroom designed for a child. All he knew were cars, campsites and cheap motels.

And Michael's farmhouse, of course. A place he was barely welcome.

Just then Heather looked past Bobby and saw Michael. He stood in the background, his expression guarded.

Justin gasped again, and Bobby kissed his chubby cheek. "You can come over and play anytime," he told the boy.

"Thank you," Heather whispered. Reed would be so pleased, so happy to know that Justin had an uncle who adored him.

Reed admired Bobby Elk, and for good reason.

He'd given Reed the same guidance he'd given Michael. Without Bobby, her brother would have been completely lost.

Somehow she knew Bobby would never pass judgment, even if she told him that Justin was Reed's son. Not that she ever would, but seeing Bobby with Justin warmed her heart just the same.

"How about some coffee? And juice for Justin?" Julianne coaxed everyone back into the living room.

Once they settled onto the Southwestern sofas, Heather gave Justin the fresh-squeezed juice and finger-combed his hair, smoothing it over his brow.

He hummed and drank his bottle, then fell asleep on the pillow beside his pony.

While he napped, Heather sipped coffee and chatted with Julianne and Bobby.

Michael, on the other hand, remained quiet for the rest of the evening. Every so often, he would search out Heather's gaze, but she had had no idea what he was thinking. No idea at all.

Five

Later that night, Heather came into the kitchen, where Michael doodled on a pad of paper, his thoughts spinning like a top.

He put down his pen and looked up at her. She'd changed into a pair of sweatpants and an oversize T-shirt. He wished she'd had the sense to wear a bra. He could see a vague outline of her breasts, the slight rise of those sensitive nipples.

"Is Justin still asleep?" he asked.

"He's out like a light."

"I guess he had a busy day."

"He hasn't been around a lot of people. We had to be careful on the run. We never knew who to trust." She sighed. "Maybe that's why he's so social. He's probably starved for as much companionship as he can get."

"He sure liked Bobby."

"Your uncle is easy to like."

"Yeah." And Michael wouldn't dare admit it, but he was hurt that the kid had chosen Bobby over him.

Heather prepared herself a cup of warm milk in the microwave. On long, winter nights she used to cook on the cast-iron stove, something that had always fascinated Michael. He'd purchased the antique appliance because he thought it suited his house. He hadn't actually intended to use it.

"Do you want to go outside?" he asked. "Maybe sit on the porch a spell?"

"Sure." She took her milk, blowing on the rim of the cup.

The air was a little cool, the moon high in the sky. A slight breeze blew, stirring scents from the night. A raccoon skittered up the live oak in the yard and ventured onto the roof of the house.

Michael loved the Texas Hill Country—the jagged cliffs, the secret caves, the rocks and water that dominated the land.

Heather's family had moved to the Hill Country when she was in fourth grade. By that time, Michael had been a rebellious sixth-grader who'd run headfirst into her brother, another rebellious sixth-grader who'd already done half the things Michael had only imagined.

Like smoke.

Damn, but he was craving a cigarette. He smoked the way some people dieted. On and off, back and forth. But he was trying to quit for good this time.

Especially after he'd learned Justin's mother was dying of lung cancer and she didn't even smoke. Somehow that seemed grossly unfair.

"I assumed we couldn't speak candidly in the

house, not after going out for the evening." He was aware that his place could have been bugged while they were gone.

"I'll do another sweep tomorrow."

He nodded, realizing how exhausting that must be for her.

"Is there something you wanted to discuss?" she asked.

"I think we should fix up the junk room as a nursery," he said, finally blurting the idea that had been nagging him half the night.

Heather's eyes grew wide. "You do?"

"Yeah, I mean, it's stupid that I have an extra bedroom filled with junk." And Justin's reaction to Brendan's room had drop-kicked his heart. All Justin had was a portable crib and a secondhand high chair. "Maybe we can put some kiddy-type pictures on the walls. And get some nice furniture. A toy box. A few toys to go in it."

"I don't have very much money left, Michael. I used my inheritance to help Reed."

"I know." He gazed at the swooping branches on the tree. "I'll pay for the nursery. And when you leave, you can take the stuff with you."

"Thank you." Her voice cracked, and he sensed she was happy and sad all at once.

Emotionally confused. The way he was.

"Who took my place?" she asked.

The question rattled his brain. Her place where? In his heart? In his bed? "What do you mean?"

"At the ranch. Who did you hire as the events coordinator?"

"No one." No one had taken her place, not anywhere, including at work. "I took the position, but Chef Gerard and his assistant help me out."

She sipped her milk. "Would you mind if I got involved again? I need a job. I can't expect you to support Justin and me while we're here."

Should he let her take over for a while? He was swamped with other duties. "I suppose it would be okay. But what are you going to do with Justin?"

"I'll take him to work with me when I can. And when I can't, I'll work at home."

He couldn't imagine lugging a kid to work, shuffling papers and coordinating fancy events between diaper changes, but women were more adventurous about these things, he supposed.

"Then you can give it a go. There's a wedding in the works I'd just as soon not deal with. You can have that account. The bride's being a royal pain in the ass, changing her mind every two seconds. Even Chef Gerard is losing patience."

"That's okay. I like coordinating weddings. I'll help the bride make her decisions."

Yeah, she liked coordinating weddings all right. So much so, she'd used a phony bridal convention as her excuse to go to California.

And now she was back, eighteen months later, with Reed's son in tow.

"Did you ever consider lying to me? Just telling me that Justin was mine?"

Her breath caught. "What? Oh, my God, no." She set her cup on the porch, nearly tipping it over.

He'd startled her with the abrupt change of topic, but he didn't give a damn. He turned to study her, to gauge her reaction. "Are you sure?"

She held his scrutinizing stare. "Yes."

Her eyes were as blue as ever, but her hair seemed lighter beneath the night sky, almost as pale as the moon.

"I had to ask," he said. "I had to know."

"Would you feel differently about him if he were your son?"

Michael didn't know how to answer that question. It seemed cruel to say yes and unrealistic to say no. "I'd have more at stake."

She smoothed a strand of her moonlit hair, and he noticed how unsteady her hand was.

"Would you have offered to marry me?"

He cleared his throat. His mouth had gone unbelievably dry. He didn't like coordinating weddings. But worse yet was considering a ceremony of his own. "Yes."

"Even if you didn't want to?"

"Yes." He frowned, feeling like a hypocrite. "You know how I feel about illegitimacy. Uncle Bobby knows how much it bothers me, too."

"Did he say something to you about it?"

"Yes, but I told him things are strained between you and I right now. I doubt he's expecting us to announce our engagement any time soon."

"But he'll expect it eventually. Won't he?"

"Probably, but there's nothing we can do about that."

She folded her unsteady hands on her lap. She sat in a weather-beaten chair, wearing baggy clothes, yet she still managed to look beautiful.

Suddenly he wished the child Heather had brought home really were his. That he was obligated to marry her, to keep her and the baby whether he wanted to or not.

But it was too late for that, he thought. Much too late.

Heather and Michael spent Thursday evening shopping for Justin's nursery.

"This place is huge," he said as they wandered the aisles. "It's like a warehouse."

"Yes." But it came highly recommended, Heather noted. Bobby and Julianne had purchased their son's furniture at Baby Bonus. "There's a lot to see."

Michael pushed Justin in his stroller, then stopped to study the child, to watch him wiggle in his seat. "How's he supposed help us pick something out? He probably can't even see from this contraption."

Heather shook her head. "I doubt he knows what he wants." How many styles of cribs could a ten-month-old decide upon?

"Sure, he does." Michael reached down and lifted the boy from his stroller. "There. That's better." He bounced Justin and made him laugh. "See? Happy already."

Justin did look cozy in Michael's arms. No one would suspect that they weren't father and son. Not with their golden skin and slightly crooked smiles. Of course, Justin owned chubby cheeks and dimples, and Michael possessed hard-edged bones and a small scar near his mouth, but they still seemed right together.

"What do you think of this?" He carried the baby toward a blue and yellow display, leaving Heather to tend to the empty stroller.

Justin didn't react. He was too busy playing with the western embroidery on Michael's shirt. Then he noticed the earring glinting through his new daddy's hair. Heather had given Michael the tiny, twisted silver hoop on his twenty-first birthday. Along with a watch he still wore and a night of lovemaking that had driven him to near madness.

"What about this instead?" He shifted to a pricey oak ensemble, decorated with cowboy carvings. "It would look good in my house."

Heather's mind drifted to sugared roses and champagne, to the four-poster bed in Michael's room. Her twenty-first birthday had been just as erotic as his. The things he'd done to her, the way he'd used his mouth, his tongue, his—

"Wow." He spun the baby around. "This is exactly what you need. Check this out, buddy. It's a pony."

Justin's head whipped up. "Pa…pa…pa."

"That's right. A rocking horse."

Michael grinned at Heather, and she banged her knee on the stroller.

Gorgeous, beautiful, wicked Michael.

He balanced Justin on the rocking horse, and the baby waved his arms. He wasn't big enough to rock by himself, but Michael helped him.

Justin squealed and laughed, and Heather caught his dimple like a kiss. She could still recall the day he was born, the day he'd slid into her waiting arms, with his dark head and skinny little limbs.

Michael grinned again. "We've got to buy this. And the oak crib and dresser, too." He lifted Justin from the spring-loaded horse. "Told ya he'd help us pick out what he wanted." He patted the child's diapered bottom. "We should try to find some carousel pictures for his room. Some rainbow ponies or something." He paused and made a curious face. "Or is that too girlish?"

She wiggled Justin's foot, shaking the little tennis shoe, wondering if she should buy him a pair of cowboy boots. "Boys like merry-go-rounds, too."

"Yeah, I guess they do." Pleased, he bounced the boy in question. "We've got to get him a new cage, too."

"Cage?"

"Playpen," he clarified. "The biggest one they make. They've got to be around here somewhere. Don't they, buddy?"

Justin looked back at the rocking horse. "Pa...pa...pa."

"Yep. That's gonna be your pony." Michael turned to Heather. "The staff at the ranch has been asking about him...about our son."

"They have?"

"They've been asking about you, too." He cleared his throat, the roughness that graveled his voice. "I told them you'd be coming back to work soon."

She intended to resume her job on Monday, to bring Justin into her old office, to explain away her absence to those bold enough to pry. "Are you concerned about it? About the staff seeing us together? Gossiping behind our backs?"

"They're already gossiping."

He placed Justin back in the stroller, and as the child whined and squirmed, protesting the confinement, Michael handed him a duck-shaped rattle from the diaper bag.

The duck flew to the floor. Patient, he picked it up and tried a set of plastic keys. When that didn't work, he resorted to a bottle.

Finally he rose to face Heather. "I'm trying to acclimate myself. To get used to all of this. But it isn't easy."

She heard Justin sucking on his bottle, humming and kicking his feet. "You're doing a good job."

"Really?" He still had the plastic keys in his hand. "Do you think Justin will like me as much as he likes my uncle?"

"I think he already does."

"He didn't the other night."

"You seem more comfortable with him now."

He shrugged, smiled a little. "Yeah, I guess so. But I'm still not changing stinky diapers."

She laughed. "Most dads say that."

"Yeah, well, this dad means it."

Heather smiled, pleased that he was slipping into his role as Justin's father, doing the best he could to appear dad-like, to win the baby's affection.

"Thank you," she said.

"For what? Buying the kid some furniture? It's no big deal."

But it was, she thought. Every effort to help Justin mattered.

As they searched for the playpen aisle, he stopped in midstride. "Did you ever get ahold of that communications guy?"

She knew he meant Reed's friend. "Yes." She'd contacted him from a pay phone in town, almost feeling as if she were still on the run, dodging strangers, looking over her shoulder. "He'll check the lines next week."

"What's taking him so long?"

"He's not from this area. He can't get out here until then."

Michael waited until another customer passed before he spoke again. "Do you really think the phones are bugged?"

"Probably. I can't imagine the mob letting it go."

Thoughtful, he studied the oversize keys. "Maybe we should fake a telephone conversation. Give those nosy bastards something worth listening to. Some hot and heavy material. Something that'll burn their ears."

Her jaw nearly dropped. "You expect me to squirm and moan on the phone for you? Knowing the mob is on the other line?"

He chuckled. "Imagine the looks on their faces when they play the tape. All those breathy little sounds you make."

The last thing she wanted was to picture a bunch of sushi-sucking mobsters gathered around Denny Halloway's pool, listening to her pant.

"You just want your ego stroked."

He moved a little closer, bumping her arm, grinning devilishly. "It wouldn't be my ego you'd be pumping, darlin'."

Oh, good grief.

"Admit it. You like the idea of turning me on. Of making me crazy."

Did she? Maybe just a little.

Okay, a lot, but that was beside the point.

"Other people do it," he said. "Julianne got lonely one night and called Bobby. Of course, this was a while ago. Before they were married."

Stunned, she widened her eyes. "How would you know?"

"Bobby told me."

"And why would he tell you something like that?"

"Because I happened to mention how curious I was

about calling one of those phone-sex lines. And he sort of laughed and said that—''

''You actually considered paying someone to talk dirty to you?'' She could only stare, could only wonder what he'd been up to since she'd been gone.

''Imagine if the mob would've heard that. They'd think I was a pervert, huh?''

Hurt and jealous, she moved away from him. ''You are.''

''Oh, yeah? Well, guess what? I'm calling you tomorrow. Bright and early from my office.'' His gaze was sharp, dark and lethal. ''When you're half naked. And still in bed.''

The following afternoon, Michael came home and found Heather on her hands and knees, digging in the dirt. Working off sexual frustration, he hoped. Stewing about the phone call he'd never made.

He walked up behind her. ''I brought you some lunch.''

She spun around and glared at him. Her jeans were smudged, and her hair was banded into a messy ponytail. Already, her skin glowed from the sun. ''I'm not hungry.''

He held up the bag. ''It's shrimp kebabs. Fresh from Chef Gerard's grill.'' He knew she thrived on the gourmet meals served at the ranch. ''And banana cream pie.''

Her nose twitched. ''I'm planting my garden.''

Another influence from the chef. The Le Cordon Bleu cook had taught her about organic gardening.

Michael turned to the baby. Justin sat in the shade in his new playpen, amusing himself with balls, blocks and squeaky toys. ''Hey, buddy.''

The kid looked up and grinned.

"What do ya say? Do you want to taste your mama's lunch? I'll bet you'll like the pie." Ignoring Heather, he opened the bag and removed the dessert.

Curious, the baby crawled to the edge of the play-pen, stood and held onto the rail. Michael dipped a plastic spoon into the creamy banana filling.

The kid accepted it greedily, swallowed and chanted "Um...um...um," before he opened his mouth for another bite.

Michael gave him a second helping, then a third. "So," he said to Heather. "What made you decide to plant a garden?"

"You know I do this every spring."

"You're only going to be here for two months. Seems like a waste of time to me."

Undaunted, she shooed off a bee, waving a gloved hand. Bees always swarmed around her hair, attracted to the color. Just like Michael was.

"It's lettuce and squash. I'll be able to harvest the plants before I leave."

"You're just trying to keep busy. Trying to get your mind off talking dirty to me."

"You wish."

"Yeah, right. You're pissed because I didn't call."

"I am not." She sat back on her heels, watched him feed Justin her pie.

He shot her a smug look, took a bite of the dessert himself, just to tick her off even more. "You are, too."

"Okay. Fine. Maybe I am. And why not?" She waved away the same persistent bee, unfazed by its stinger. "You left me hanging. Fretting all morning. Afraid you'd keep calling until I answered."

But he hadn't called at all. And somehow that was worse. A rejection, he supposed. "I wasn't serious about the mob listening in."

"Yes, you were."

"Okay. Fine." He used her line, her haughty admission. "Can you blame me? I'm tired of looking like the jilted boyfriend. The jerk who waited around for you."

"You didn't wait."

"You think I had sex with other women?"

"If you didn't, you sure thought about it."

"Of course I thought about it. You were gone for eighteen months. A year and a half," he punctuated, digging into the pie again.

She tore off her gloves. "I didn't think about sleeping with other men."

Great. Now she was going to lay a guilt trip on him. "How was I supposed to know that? You took off. You left. No card. No phone call. No see ya later, chump."

Justin whined, and Michael realized the kid waited for another bite, the spoonfuls he'd been shoveling into his own mouth. "Sorry, buddy."

Heather snorted. "If he gets hyper from all that sugar, I'm making you stay up with him tonight."

"Like I've got anything else to do." But head to the nearest bar, he thought. Drown his loneliness in beer. "I should have gotten laid. I should've found a new lover. Gotten my rocks off good and tight."

Ice edged her voice, cold and crisp. "So why didn't you?"

"Because I missed you. *You,*" he all but snarled. His obsession. The blonde he couldn't seem to get out of his system. "And I didn't want to deal with a bunch of emotional crap from someone else.'' When you take a woman to bed, she thinks she owns you, he thought. Or you start thinking you own her, pining for her day and night, the way he'd done with Heather. ''Women are a pain in the ass.''

She smoothed her misbehaving ponytail, locked those stunning blue eyes onto his. A small breeze rustled her blouse, molding the light cotton material against her body.

''You missed me that much?''

''I just said I did, didn't I?'' A damn fool admission he wished he could retract.

Her gaze didn't waver. She didn't blink, didn't look away from him. ''So what did you do?''

''About what?''

''Sex.''

He glanced at her breasts, at her peaking nipples, then cursed himself for noticing, for caring.

What in the hell did she think he did? Took up pinochle? ''I got drunk and watched porn,'' he shot back.

She gasped. ''You didn't.''

''Oh, yes I did.'' Her puritan reaction had him grinning, especially after all the erotic things they used to do to each other. ''I've got an adult film collection that would curl your toes.''

''Oh, my.'' Miss Innocent simply sat and stared.

He chuckled and tossed her the bag of kebabs. ''Eat your shrimp, little girl. And later, I'll treat you to a movie.''

She caught the bag, and they both laughed.

''You're evil, Michael.''

"And you're still wishing I would have called."

"Maybe." She slid a shrimp from the stick and sucked on it, letting him know that somewhere deep down, she was blessedly evil, too.

Six

"**H**eather?"

She heard Michael's voice, almost as though it drifted through a fog. Then she shifted on the sofa and realized she'd dozed off.

"I'm done."

She sat up and squinted, forcing her mind to catch up with her body. "Done?"

"With Justin's room."

Her brain kicked into gear. Michael had worked all weekend on the nursery. He'd continued to shop, to have more furniture delivered, to haul in smaller items on his own, to put the finishing touches on what she'd yet to see.

He wanted to surprise Justin, and that meant surprising her, too.

She glanced at the clock. It was after ten on Sunday

night. "I put Justin to bed over an hour ago. Chester went with him."

"Oh." Disappointed, he sat on the sofa beside her. "I didn't realize it was so late. I guess I lost track of time."

"I can wake him."

"No. That's okay." He turned to look at her, expectation shining in his dark eyes. "Do you want to see it?"

"Are you kidding? It's all I could do not to peek in on you. I'm dying to see it." She'd been lurking outside the door for days, listening to the noises within, the shuffle of his feet, the clank of his hammer.

He smiled and rose from the couch, encouraging her to do the same. "It's actually pretty cool."

She followed him into the room, then stopped dead in her tracks. "Oh, Michael."

Cool didn't begin to describe what he'd done.

He'd decorated every corner, every crevice, every open space. The lamp on the dresser beamed with cowboy silhouettes, figures that matched the carvings on the crib. A kid-size couch sported cozy pillows and the toy box overflowed with cars, trucks and funny little farm animals.

And the pictures on the walls. "You found them." The carousel horses they'd talked about. Painted ponies, with flowing manes and dancing hoofs.

"I almost gave up. Then I got on-line and made a mad search."

And probably paid a fortune to have them shipped overnight. "This is beautiful. All of it." The ornate oak shelves he'd added, the leather recliner, the calf-printed curtains, the vintage cowboy boots nailed around the doorframe, the dream catcher, with its careful webbing and beaded feathers dangling over the crib.

The rocking horse, she noticed, had acquired a mate. A smaller, simpler wooden pony Justin could reach by himself.

"You can take everything with you," he said. "Except the curtains, I guess. Unless they fit your next window."

She didn't want to think about leaving. She wanted to focus on being here, in Michael's house. "Justin is going to be thrilled."

"I hope so." He hooked his thumbs in his pockets, a stance far more casual than his emotions allowed. "I don't want him to feel like a secondhand kid. Not now. And certainly not later."

Once again, she fought the future, the reality of raising Justin by herself. "Later is a long ways off."

"Not that long."

"He's still a baby."

"He'll be walking soon. Then talking. Then wondering about his dad." Michael tapped the smaller pony with his foot and sent it rocking. "About me."

She watched the wooden horse make a graceful bow, then lift its head. "Yes, you." The father of the baby that had died. The infant with no heartbeat. No pulse.

"What about when he's old enough to comprehend the truth? Are you going to tell him about his real parents?"

"Reed and Beverly don't want him to know. Not unless it's absolutely necessary. If there's a medical emergency or if you decide you can't handle—"

"We'll deal with that when the time comes. But I

plan on sending money when you need it. When you get settled.''

She held his gaze, knowing his wouldn't falter. She could see kindness in his eyes, the tough-guy tenderness that made him who he was.

God forgive me, she thought. For not telling him about his son. "This isn't about money, Michael.''

"I know.''

But it mattered to him, she realized. Justin's well-being mattered. "He's going to respect you.''

The pony stopped rocking. "How can he if I'm not around?''

"Then I'll tell him the truth. I won't let him think ill of you.''

Michael frowned. "My dad was a bastard. Your dad was a bastard. And so was Reed's. We all got the shaft.''

Childhood images surfaced. Her father bellowing about his rotten stepson, her brother slamming out the door, her mother chain-smoking in front of the TV, Heather scurrying around the kitchen like a mouse, washing dishes and praying she didn't break one.

"I think it was worse for you,'' he said. "Reed barely remembers his real dad, and I never met mine. But you tried to please yours.''

"I was glad when he left. When he walked out on us.'' Yet her frantic, flighty mother had begged him to stay, mourning his absence for the rest of her anxiety-ridden life. "It'll be different for Justin.'' She placed her hand on the crib, gripped the wood. "It already is.''

He blew a breath. "I didn't mean to bring up all that junk. To upset you.''

"I'm not upset. How can I be?'' She lifted her

mood, the dark veil floating over her heart. She'd spent too many nights dwelling on the past, too many long, shiftless hours wondering why her father had been cruel and demanding, why her mother had taken his side, why her brother had gotten tangled up in the mob, why the baby she'd given birth to had died. "Look at this room. Look at the magic you created." She stepped forward, reached out to hug him. "It's incredible."

He accepted her embrace. And suddenly, everything changed.

Heat swirled low in her belly. He ran his hands down her back and pressed his body closer to hers.

She held on to his shoulders; he nuzzled her neck.

Memories filtered through her mind—the first time they'd made love. The first time he'd unbuttoned her blouse, unhooked her bra, unzipped her jeans, slid his hand down her panties.

She tipped her head back. "I wish…"

"Me, too." He brushed his lips over her skin.

Unable to stop herself, she rubbed against him. He was tall and hard and virile. Familiar, yet not.

He seemed stronger, a little older, more intense. She could feel his muscles bunch beneath her fingers.

"Tell me what you miss the most," he said.

"I…"

"Tell me."

She closed her eyes, fought a wave of dizziness. "Your hands. Your mouth." He licked the shell of her ear, and her knees went weak. "Your tongue."

"Foreplay," he whispered.

"Yes." And being in love, she thought. Of allowing herself to fall under his spell. Of dreaming that they were meant to be.

He brought his face next to hers. And for a moment, for one silent, life-altering moment, neither moved.

Then he kissed her.

So hard, so rough, so desperately, she imagined climbing all over him, devouring him inch by inch.

He pushed his hands through her hair, wound it around his fingers, twining and turning, tugging her head back a little more. "I missed being inside you. The warmth. The wetness. All that hot, slick…"

She felt his pulse hammer, the rush of masculine excitement. He missed the orgasm, the final release, the surge of his body spilling into hers.

"Come to my room." He kissed her again. "Be with me."

She wanted to, more than anything. "For how long?"

"I don't know. I can't think about that. Not now." He held her, gently, reverently. "I can't make promises. I never could."

His admission stabbed her heart; yet his touch, those warm, capable hands, belied his words. "You confuse me."

"I need you, Heather."

She buried her face against his chest. It hurt *not* to be with him, *not* to have him. "I need you, too. So help me, I do."

That was all it took. He scooped her into his arms and carried her to his room, shouldering his way into the open doorway.

His bed was unmade from the night before, sheets tangled, pillowcases twisted.

She looked around, saw the whirlwind that was Michael: clothes piled in the corner, an empty beer bottle

on the dresser, coins scattered, five-dollar bills folded
and crumpled.

He deposited her on the bed and followed her
down. A night-light burned, shadowing the room in
golden hues. When his hair fell across his forehead,
he pushed it back, away from his face.

That strong, angular face.

She looked into his eyes and met his gaze, the dark
desire, the power he wielded over her.

Michael Damian Elk, with the slashing eyebrows
and slow, determined smile.

This was dangerous, she thought. Letting him take
what he wanted. Letting him—

As he went after her blouse, his voice rasped, graz-
ing each syllable. "Heath-er. Sweet, sex-y…"

Michael. Her Michael. "Don't stop," she told him.
Not now. Not ever.

"I won't." He popped the third button, cursed and
fumbled with the next one.

She yanked at his shirt, dragging it from his pants.

They rolled over the bed, groping, grasping, tearing
off clothes and tossing them onto the floor.

Greed lashed through her system, quick and feral,
like the snap of a whip, the brand of leather against
skin.

His flesh was hot and hard, gloriously male. But he
didn't let her touch him, not nearly enough.

Instead he pushed her onto the bed, lifted her hips
and lowered his head.

To drive her crazy. To flay her to madness.

Lifting her legs onto his shoulders, he pulled her
closer, using his mouth, his tongue, a clever nip of
teeth.

She arched. She bucked. She sizzled.

He knew what this did to do her; knew it made her mindless; knew his ministrations made her crave him.

All of him. Deep inside her.

Scraping a hand across the ridge of his cheekbone, the slant of his jaw, Heather gulped the air in her lungs.

"I want you." She tried to pull him up, but he resisted.

"Not yet."

No, not yet. He wasn't done with her yet. He—

A shiver racked her body. Sensation sliced sensation, battering her senses. He kept licking, tasting, spurring her on.

Until she exploded.

Until she cried his name and clawed his shoulders, until the pleasure left her molten and weak, dizzy and dazed.

And desperate, so incredibly desperate, for the man she loved.

Michael wanted her like this, just like this, coming unglued before his eyes. Her hair spilled everywhere, down her arms, over her breasts, across the bed.

He rose to straddle her, to poise above her, to watch the last shuddering wave of her orgasm.

Her eyes locked onto his, and she reached for him, stroking between his legs. He couldn't get any harder. He was already fully aroused, seeping moisture at the tip.

She rubbed the pearly bead into his skin, and he kissed her.

Heather was every blonde he saw, every erotic actress in the movies he watched, every long, leggy model in a centerfold, on a bikini calendar.

His fantasy.

His obsession.

He kissed her again, rougher this time. She dug her ragged nails into his back, giving him more of the same.

And then he plunged into her.

Wet and slick, she welcomed him, drawing him deeper, coveting what they both needed. Wanted. Craved.

A year and a half, he thought. Eighteen torturous months of celibacy.

He moved; she moved with him.

Synchronicity. It had always been like this, from the moment he'd taken her virginity, from the instant she'd offered him her innocence.

He'd cherished her then. He cherished her now.

And hated himself for it.

No woman should do to a man what she did to him.

Michael pumped harder, setting a fast, driving rhythm. Animal sex. Human lust. The lines were blurring, misting his vision, graying the edges of sanity.

She wrapped her legs around him, and he rode her, telling himself not to fall in love. Not to let her bewitch him.

She reared up to drag his mouth to hers, to tease his tongue, to nip his bottom lip, to use her magic, her power.

He wanted to curse, to damn them both to hell. But he held her instead, letting her heartbeat pummel his.

Heather. Sweet, sexy Heather.

How had he survived all this time without her?

Passion, fresh and powerful, slammed through his veins. She put her hands all over him, across his chest, down his abdomen, between his legs as he moved in and out of her body.

She knew how to turn him on, how to bring him to that climatic peak.

And he was close, so damn close.

He closed his eyes, and she whispered in his ear. Erotic words. Words that sent fire streaking through his blood.

He thrust deeper. Into the obsession, the fantasy, the woman he'd tried so desperately to forget.

And finally, as he battled for relief, for the vicious war to end, he spilled his seed and collapsed in her arms.

She stroked his back, gliding feather-light fingertips over sweat-dampened skin.

He stayed there for a moment, breathing in her scent, the blend of strawberries and sex, summer fruit and spring lust.

Then he lifted his head and rolled onto his side, taking her with him. He wasn't ready to let her go. Not yet.

Stretching and mewling, she gave him a satisfied smile, like a kitten that just had lapped its weight in cream.

He drew a lazy circle around one of her nipples and watched it rise. Michael knew Heather liked the aftermath of an orgasm, the simple pleasure of being naked and spent.

She'd taught him to like it, too. To cuddle, to talk, to make the intimacy last.

And when it lasted beyond his limit, he simply took her again. Which, to him, was part of the mating ritual. The guy part, he supposed.

Suddenly his brain kicked into another gear. "Did

we just blow it?'' Protection hadn't even occurred to
him. But he didn't have a condom available anyway.
Not one that wasn't expired.

"I'm on the Pill."

The breath he'd been holding rushed out. Then he
tilted his head, curious. "You stayed on it all this
time?"

"No. I saw a doctor before I came here."

"Because you figured this would happen?"

She looked away for a second. "I wasn't sure. I
didn't know what to expect."

But she was prepared nonetheless. She'd used the
Pill throughout most their relationship. Of course,
she'd switched prescriptions a few times, struggling
with some of the side effects, but she'd always ex-
perienced drug sensitivities. Aspirin burned her stomach, antibiotics made her queasy.

"I was hoping," she said.

"That we'd have sex?"

"That you'd take me back."

Which wasn't the same thing, he thought. "This
isn't a reconciliation."

"I know. You already told me. No promises."

"And no regrets." Guilty, he skimmed her cheek.
Did she have to look so soft, so angelic? So mortally
wounded? "Let's take one day at a time." He tipped
her chin, encouraged her to meet his gaze. "Okay?"

She chewed her lip, put her head on his shoulder.
"Okay."

He smoothed a hand down her hair. "You can
move into my room if you want to."

"So we can keep having sex?"

"That's always been good between us."

She snuggled closer. "Just good?"

"Great. Incredible." He sketched a finger down her spine, then cupped her bottom and drew her tight against him, grateful she wasn't going to dwell on being melancholy. "The best."

She made a breathy sound. "That feels good."

"Just good?"

"Great. Incredible."

She lifted her head to kiss him, and the heat started rising. In his loins, in his heart.

Michael closed his eyes, then said her name, just once, before he made love to her all over again.

The alarm clocked shrieked in Heather's ear. She climbed over Michael to turn it off. He stirred, moaned and rolled over.

Heather couldn't resist watching him sleep. A sheet draped his waist, pooling between his legs. His chest and stomach were exposed, and his hair covered half of his face.

She'd missed the allure of waking up beside a rumpled male, inhaling his scent, locking on to the sexual pheromones emanating from his body.

Beautiful Michael.

He didn't like being called beautiful, but she couldn't help thinking of him that way.

Snuggling into the morning, she kissed his shoulder, then traced the ebony ink on his arm, following the primitive shapes. He'd designed the tattoo during his teenage years, but it was more than an artistic rebellion. The tribal mark was his way of embracing his heritage, of taking pride in a culture he used to shun.

He opened his eyes and squinted at her. "Is it time to get up already?"

"Six a.m."

"Damn." He snaked his arm out and grabbed her. She landed on top of him with a feminine squeal and a heart-skipping thud.

He pinched her bottom, and they laughed and rolled over the bed, untangling the sheet and putting flesh-to-flesh.

His arousal pressed her stomach, the silky hardness warm and inviting.

"Happy to see me?" she asked, skimming the tip, making his body jump.

"That happens every morning. Or did you forget?"

No, she hadn't forgotten. She remembered everything about him. Every dark, dangerous detail.

"In that case." She tried to roll away, but he held her good and tight.

"Okay. I give. I'm happy to see you." He dragged her mouth to his, and before she could draw breath, she was pinned beneath him.

Cuffing her wrists with his hands, he held her arms above her head.

Then the baby cried. A wailing scream that sent them scrambling like guilty lovers, like a couple who'd gotten caught in the throes of a forbidden affair.

Was that what this was? she wondered. A forbidden affair? A secret rendezvous?

"I'll get him." Sorting through the pile of clothes on the floor, Heather grabbed her blouse.

A second later, Justin fell silent.

Too silent.

She pulled on her panties. "He never does that. He never stops crying until someone gets him up."

"Do you think something's wrong?"

"I don't know." She rushed out the door, Michael on her heels. She heard him stumbling into his jeans, attacking his zipper with clumsy hands.

They found Justin standing in his portable crib, grinning his fool head off, smacking the top of Chester's furry head.

Michael chuckled. "Looks like he has a new nursemaid."

"So it seems." Heather's heart quit pounding. She'd forgotten that the dog had slept at the foot of Justin's bed last night.

Michael reached for the baby. "You little hyena. You scared the shi—" he paused to reword his phrase "—stuffing out of us." Another sudden pause. "Damn. He's soaked. Here." He handed the responsibility to Heather. "I haven't got the diaper-thing down yet."

"You haven't even tried."

"So sue me. I'm not used to being a dad. And this is only temporary, remember?"

How could she forget? No promises. No regrets.

She changed Justin, and he kicked his feet and tried to work himself free, determined to pet Chester again.

The dog sniffed the wet diaper, and Michael swatted him. "Come on. Have some manners." He reached for the baby again. "Hey, buddy. Want to see your new room?"

With Chester in tow, they headed to the nursery. Justin gasped and flailed his arms, and the dog hopped onto the kid-size couch, deciding it was meant for him.

"Pa...pa...pa!"

"Yep. Your pony's here. Two ponies."

Michael spun the child around, and Heather watched them. Her lover. Her son.

God help her, but she wanted to keep both of them. Forever.

Seven

Heather loved Elk Ridge Ranch. She thrived on the colorful pastures, the sparkling streams and the long, winding horse trails.

The prestigious ranch accommodated a variety of guests, offering rustic cabins in the hills or luxurious rooms in the lodge. The lodge itself housed a gym, a masseuse, a hair salon, a gift shop, a new clothing boutique, a dining room and an indoor pool. On moonlit evenings, an outdoor pool invited a sea of stars, flutes of champagne and gourmet appetizers.

"Are you nervous?" Michael asked.

She sat next to him in his truck, with Justin babbling in the extended cab. "A little." What woman wouldn't be on her first day back at the job? "But I'm excited, too." Happy to return to the place that could only be described as home.

She adjusted the sterling silver barrette in her hair.

She'd chosen a tan dress and sleek brown boots, opting for western professional. "Do you think people are going to ask where I've been?"

Michael parked the vehicle and swung open his door. "I don't know. Some might, but I'm pretty sure my uncle already spread the word."

Her pulse raced. "What word?"

"That Reed was hiding from some criminals, and you were with him." He watched her remove Justin from the car seat. "I didn't mention who those criminals were."

She tried for a casual air. "The Mafia isn't as prevalent as it used to be."

"But they're still out there."

"Yes." Men like Denny Halloway still existed, tough, ambitious men restoring the roots of organized crime, living by their own set of rules.

They climbed the wraparound porch, with Michael lugging the diaper bag and cumbersome playpen. Heather carried Justin, and the baby looked around, his eyes big and curious. He'd bawled like crazy when they'd taken him out of his new room, but he'd finally settled into another adventure.

Going to work with Mommy and Daddy.

His new mommy and daddy, she amended. Before this, she had been his aunt and Michael had been a stranger.

She hugged the baby a little closer, pressing her cheek to his. In spite of Justin's inability to express himself through words, she knew he hadn't forgotten Beverly and Reed. But eventually he would, and that made her hurt for the boy's parents.

Heather cleared her mind and entered the lodge, taking in the lobby. Immediately, warmth and beauty surrounded her. Oak walls, a stone fireplace, floor-to-ceiling windows and hand-crafted furniture presented Texas comfort at its finest.

The lodge was quiet, but within the hour Elk Ridge's guests would be filtering into the dining area for a country meal.

"Oh, *mi preciosa!*"

Heather looked up to see Maria Sandoval racing toward her. Maria, the receptionist at the lodge, had mothered Heather when no one else would.

The Latina woman, sporting a brightly colored dress and salt-and-pepper hair, gathered Heather and Justin in a sturdy hug. Heather nearly melted in her arms, grateful for the genuine welcome.

Maria stepped back to view the baby, then clutched a hand to her heart. "So sweet. So perfect. He looks like Señor Michael, no?" Tilting her head, she tapped Justin's nose. "But he looks like you, too. Like both of you."

Did Reed and Beverly's son resemble her and Michael? "Thank you." Heather smiled. "I missed you, Maria."

"And now you're home. Now you'll stay, no?"

Heather didn't get the chance to respond. Michael stepped forward, making more noise than necessary. "I'm going to haul this stuff to your office," he said to Heather, shifting the diaper bag and rattling the playpen.

Maria watched him go. "He was lonely without you, *señorita*. So lonely. But angry sometimes, too."

"I didn't mean to stay away."

"I know. I heard." The receptionist squeezed her hand. "You go now. You work. And I'll have the chef send some breakfast. For the baby, too."

Heather's office looked the same. A mahogany desk faced the window and two tall file cabinets dominated a blank wall. The other walls presented artwork she'd chosen, paintings that depicted wishing wells, stone castles and gazebos by the shore.

"I left the files you'll need on your desk," Michael said. "But you'll have to call Lorraine if you need any help. I'll be tied up most of the day."

"That's okay." She'd always enjoyed working with the chef's assistant. "I like Lorraine."

"And you like being back."

"Yes, I do."

Her eyes sought his, and they stared at each other, their lovemaking attempt from this morning suddenly drifting between them.

"I better go," he said.

She placed Justin in the playpen, wondering if Michael would kiss her goodbye.

He did. Gently, ever so gently.

Then he ruffled the baby's hair and left quietly, closing the door on his way out.

Michael returned to Heather's office at three o'clock and found it empty. Silent. Almost ghostly.

A blast of loneliness slammed into his gut. A physical reminder of the eighteen months he'd lived without her.

Don't, he told himself. Don't start missing her all over again. Let her go this time, move on with your life once she and Justin are gone.

Capping his emotions, Michael closed Heather's door, preparing to return to work, to delve into the spreadsheets stacked in his office. He didn't mind handling the books. He'd always been gifted with numbers. Of course, he preferred being outdoors, but he spent plenty of dude-ranch days hosting barn dances, hayrides and picnics.

Activities Heather used to attend with him.

As he neared the lobby, he slowed his pace. It wouldn't hurt to ask Maria what time Heather had left, why she'd cut out early, who'd driven her to the farmhouse.

He had a right to know. Didn't he?

He waited for Maria to complete a transaction with a guest before he moved forward.

"Señor Michael." She greeted him in her heavy accent. She'd been manning the reception desk at Elk Ridge since its inception, treating him with respect, even when he was a whiskey-rousing teenager.

"Hey." He gave her a charming smile, wondering if she simply considered him a whiskey-rousing adult. He'd curbed his boyhood ways, but over the past eighteen months, he'd partied, a bit severely at times, to forget the pain.

"When did she leave?" he asked, hating himself for not being able to erase her from his mind.

"Who?" Maria cocked her head. "Oh, you mean Señorita Heather? About an hour ago." Her brow creased in thought. "Justin was getting fussy. Not that he wasn't a good boy. But he's only a baby, no? Too much excitement for one day."

"Who took them home?"

"Señor Bobby."

Michael merely nodded. Trust his uncle to be available when he wasn't. "I better get back to work." He tapped the top of the reception desk, signaling his departure.

A moment later, his departure took him away from the lodge and into the crisp Hill Country air.

He damned himself for wanting to see Heather and Justin, for wanting to hear about their day. But he ditched the mile-high spreadsheets and drove to the farmhouse anyway.

The familiar path led him past towering trees and flowering landscape.

Once his house came into view, he steered down the long, graveled driveway and squinted at the figures on his porch. Heather and two suited men.

The communications expert wasn't due until tomorrow, and he was supposed to be dressed like a telephone repairman. So who were the suits?

He spotted their car, a white sedan, parked inconspicuously by the side of the house.

Heather didn't appear the least bit comfortable. Her arms were crossed, her entire body language tense.

Michael spun his tires, spitting gravel. Heather and the suits turned, and he saw a look of relief on her face.

He jammed the vehicle into Park and squared his shoulders, ready to defend the woman he was sleeping with, to come to her rescue.

He took the porch steps, and Heather said his name.

"Michael." Her voice was soft, just above a whisper.

He brushed her cheek with a lover's kiss and faced the suits, letting them know he was willing to do battle.

For a moment no one spoke, then Michael addressed the older of the two men, a distinguished city slicker with graying temples and a dark jacket.

"You mind telling me who you are?"

The intruder flashed a badge and an ID. "Special Agent Sims."

FBI?

Well, hell. Michael paused, studied the shield, the government ID. "I happen to be Michael Elk. And this is my house. My ranch." Ending the introduction, he moved closer to Heather. "My woman."

Sims inclined his head. "Yes, we've met Miss Richmond." He indicated his partner. "Myself and Special Agent Hoyt."

Michael spared Hoyt a glance. Young thirties, red-dish blond hair, cheap tie slightly askew.

He turned back to Sims. "So what's this all about?"

The older man kept a professional stance, a controlled demeanor. "We were hoping Miss Richmond could help us locate Reed Blackwood."

Michael swore beneath his breath, felt Heather shift uncomfortably beside him.

"We're aware that Mr. Blackwood is affiliated with the West Coast Family," Sims said.

"Is Reed under investigation?" Michael asked.

"We're interested in his association with Denny Halloway."

Heather's blue eyes turned smoky. "I already told you, I don't know where Reed is."

"Your brother is in trouble, Miss Richmond." Special Agent Hoyt put in his two cents, then straightened his tie, his sun-sensitive skin chaffed from the wind. "And you better hope we find him before Halloway does."

Taking offense, Michael stepped forward. "Where the hell was the FBI when I filed a missing persons report? When Heather and her brother disappeared?

Why didn't anyone tell me then that Reed was involved with the mob? That my lady was in the thick of it?''

Hoyt, much to his credit, held his ground, even though Michael did his damnedest to back the shorter, slightly built agent against the porch rail.

"We weren't aware that Mr. Blackwood was part of the West Coast Family then.''

"He ran off with the boss's daughter.''

"At the time, his personal association with Miss Halloway didn't place him as a member of her father's organization.''

But something did, Michael thought. An investigation they were currently working on.

Sims took charge again. He handed Heather a business card, and when she refused to accept it, he offered it to Michael.

"We believe we can help Mr. Blackwood.''

"How?'' Michael snapped the card out of the agent's hand.

"We would prefer to discuss that with Mr. Blackwood. So if you hear from him, if he should contact you, please refer him to us.''

With that, Sims smiled briefly, thanking them for their time and bidding them a good day. Hoyt did neither. He followed his partner to their car, leaving Michael and Heather alone.

The white sedan backed out of its sheltered spot and headed down the graveled driveway, disappearing into a white speck in the distance.

Heather's knees went weak, her bones turning to slush. Michael remained beside her, strong and tall in a denim shirt and cowboy-cut jeans. Her rock. Her protector.

She breathed the floral-scented air, desperate to get a grip on her fear, to keep her legs from buckling beneath her. "How can we be sure they're who they say they are?"

He turned, a frown marring his brow. "You think they were a couple of Halloway's men posing as FBI?"

"Anything is possible." Anything at all, she thought.

Michael studied the card in his hand. "I'll check it out. I'll make sure they're who they claim to be."

"I just wish this would end." But how could it? Her brother would be hunted for the rest of his life, and she would continue to look over her shoulder, to doubt everyone who came her way.

"Let's go inside." Michael opened the door, slipped the business card in his wallet. "Where's Justin?"

"Taking a nap. But I think I should check on him." To watch him sleep, to pray that he remained hers to keep.

Together, she and Michael entered the baby's room, and Heather inched closer to the crib. Justin's eyes were closed, his legs curled under him, his padded bottom in the air. The naptime bottle she'd given him was half-full, and his pony lay at his side, its gold-streaked mane sparkling in the afternoon light.

She glanced at the dream catcher above the crib. Would it protect Justin? Trap the bad dreams in the webbing and send the good ones into the feathers? Save them to be dreamt again?

"I wonder if he dreams about ponies," she said.

Michael kept his voice hushed. "Has he ever seen a real horse?"

"Not up close."

"Then we'll take him to the barn soon. He'll like that, don't you think?"

"Yes." Her heart turned spongy, and she soaked up the moment, the man, the wishing-well hope of being a family.

"Come on." Michael edged his way to the door. "We better go before we wake him up."

Leaving Justin to his dreams, they found themselves in the kitchen, brewing coffee and warming croissants.

"I came home to see how your day went," Michael said, adding too many coffee grounds to the filter.

"Aside from Sims and Hoyt, it went well."

"Maria said Justin was fussy."

"Just a little." Now the memory made her ache. He'd crawled on the floor in her office, tugged on phone cords, knocked over the trash and whined for her attention. Next time she would bounce him on her lap instead of losing patience and carting him home. "He'll settle into the routine. He'll get used to my office."

Michael filled the carafe with water. He made a terrible pot of coffee, but at the moment, she didn't care. All that mattered was being near him.

"Thank you," she said.

He leaned against the counter. "For what?"

For treating Reed's son with care, for standing up to those men, for calling her his woman. "For being my friend." She met his gaze, held it, treasured it. "And my lover."

"Believe me, that's my pleasure."

He moved closer, and suddenly they forgot about

the coffee, about buttering the croissants, about everything except each other.

They kissed all the way to the bedroom, then stumbled onto the four-poster bed, kicking off boots, peeling off clothes.

As she attacked the snaps on his shirt, he managed the delicate buttons on her blouse and went after the front clasp on her bra, flicking it open. The zipper on her skirt proved easy enough, but the panty hose had him yanking and tugging.

He cursed, and she laughed. "Let me help."

Her panties came next. His jeans and boxers followed.

In a moment of calm, they held each other, pressing close. Sunlight spilled over the bed, and he rubbed against her, creating more warmth.

More copper-skinned heat.

Heather roamed his body, fascinated by the cords of muscle. Losing herself in memories, she circled his nipples, flattened her palms on the center of his chest, traced a finger down his stomach. She wanted to tell him how much she loved him, but she feared the words would trouble him so she let them drift, flutter like leaves falling to the ground.

He slid his hands into her hair. "I want you."

"Me first." She kissed his navel, and his breath rushed out, sending erotic shivers up and down her spine.

"What are you doing to me?" he asked, even though they both knew.

She moved lower, teasing him with her tongue. The gentle hands in her hair turned rough, cupping the back of her head, pulling her closer.

Heather's blood swam, her heart pounded at her

throat. She wanted this as badly as he did—the lash of pleasure, the searing brand of mouth to body.

Sensation slid over skin, over smooth, hard flesh. She set the rhythm, the sweet, rocking motion.

He watched her, his eyes much too intense.

Empowered, she took him deeper. Deeper than she'd ever taken him before.

He fisted the sheets and made a tortured sound, battling the need for relief.

Teasing, playing, she kissed her way up his body. She'd dreamed about him like this, just like this, warm and fluid, hard and hungry, all dark and male.

Michael. Beautiful, desperate Michael.

Without warning, he gripped her waist, lifted her hips and thrust into her, sending shock waves rippling.

"Do it," he rasped against her ear. "Make it happen."

A pulse pounded between her legs. Heat slammed through every inch of her body. The room spun in a sea of color, a blur of skyrocketing emotion.

She rode him, fast and hard, furious to climax with him. To make it happen.

He moved with her, baiting her, arousing her, covering her mouth and devouring it.

Demanding, persuasive, he took her to dangerous heights, and she knew she would never stop needing him, wanting him, craving him.

He was in her blood, in her heart, in her soul.

When he flung back his head and lost the battle, she let herself go, tumbling over the edge and falling into his arms.

In the silence that followed, he held her, steeped in the aftermath of a mind-reeling climax. Slick with sweat, with the sheen of completion, she cuddled closer.

"I can't do this," he said.

She smoothed a hand down his back. Her limbs had turned to liquid and her fingers melted like wax. "Do what?"

"Stay. Snuggle. Get turned on again." He slid his hands through her hair and made an approving sound, lingering over the long, loose strands.

She knew the platinum color fascinated him, just as the inky blackness that streamed to his shoulders mesmerized her. "Why can't you stay?"

"Because I have to go back to work."

"What about later?"

"We'll snuggle. Kiss. Get turned on again."

She brushed his neck with her lips, tasted the saltiness of his skin. "After I feed you?"

"Feed me?"

"Dinner."

"That's sounds perfect." He shifted to ease her out of his arms. "I'll bring my appetite. For you. And your cooking."

She smiled and touched his cheek, and he gave her a tender kiss and left her alone.

Anxious for him to return.

Michael came home from work, expecting to find Heather bustling around the stove, preparing a mouth-watering meal.

A pot roast, he decided, as he opened the front door. Or maybe a vat of spaghetti.

He entered the kitchen, and his hungry stomach sank.

Nothing, not the slightest aroma laced the air. No sizzling meats, no spices, no tangy sauces.

He searched for Heather and discovered her in Justin's room, leaning against the dresser.

She seemed distracted, edgy. Glancing up to meet his gaze, she wrung her hands, locking her fingers, then pulling them apart.

Justin sat on the floor, amid a batch of toys, while Chester chewed a piece of rawhide. Spotting Michael, the dog thumped his bushy tail.

Michael moved farther into the room. Was Heather angry with him? Had he done something to displease her?

"What's going on?" he asked.

She caught her breath but didn't answer.

The sound of Michael's voice triggered Justin's attention, and the little one crawled toward him, babbling baby nonsense.

"Hey, buddy." He lifted the child into his arms, still waiting for Heather's response.

Justin latched onto Michael's shirt and tugged on the collar. The boy smelled clean and powdery, freshly bathed and shampooed.

"Say something, Heather." Anything, he thought, as he pressed his cheek to Justin's hair, allowing the softness to tickle his skin.

"Denny Halloway called."

His heartbeat slammed his chest. "When?"

"Not long after you left."

"What did he want?"

"For me to come to California."

Afraid of losing her, of her going to L.A. and never coming back, he shook his head. "No. You can't." It was too dangerous, too risky, too everything.

"Beverly's dying, Michael. She probably won't last the week."

"Is that what he told you? Was that his ploy to lure you back there?" He held the baby a little closer, a little tighter. "What if it's a ruse? What if he found out about Justin? What if—"

"He said Beverly wants to see me. That she's been asking for me."

"And you believe him?"

She wrung her hands again. "I don't know, but it's a chance I have to take. If Beverly is on her deathbed, then she has a right to see me. To see her son one last time."

"And tip off her father?" Overly possessive, he clutched the child he'd agreed to claim. "I won't let you go. You're both staying here."

She lifted her chin, gave him a stubborn stare. "I'm flying out as soon as I can. And I'm taking Justin with me."

He wanted to curse, to scream, to accuse her of being selfish. Yet he knew she was doing this for Beverly, for a young woman riddled with cancer.

"I'll go with you." No way would he let her disappear on her own, take the baby and run, put herself in harm's way. "But we're waiting a day."

"What good will—"

He cut off her argument, stating his case. "The communication expert is checking the phone lines tomorrow. We can't bail while he's here. And I still have to find out if Sims and Hoyt are who they say they are."

She backed down. "How are you going to do that?"

"I'll go to a local FBI office and ask them to verify

what we need to know.'' According to the card
stuffed in Michael's wallet, Sims and Hoyt hailed
from California, but that didn't mean a Texas branch
couldn't help.

"Does it matter who they are?" she asked.

"It might matter to Reed. They claimed they could
help your brother."

Her eyes clouded. "Maybe, but I'm not sure who
to trust anymore. Who to believe."

"I know." He moved closer, taking Justin with
him, wondering what the next few days would bring.

If he and Heather were headed for danger.

For a trap Denny Halloway had sprung.

Eight

The California sun shone bright. Palm trees loomed to the sky, residing over the prestigious neighborhood with a tropical air.

Denny Halloway's West L.A. house, shrouded by greenery and a wrought-iron gate, presided like a grand illusion, barely visible from the street.

"So this is it." Michael stopped the rented SUV, apprehensive about entering the driveway.

Heather shifted in her seat. "Yes, this is it."

The final charade, he thought. Or the final curtain. He glanced back at the baby. Justin sat in a car seat, clutching his pony and kicking his feet. His thick dark hair was neatly combed, and his chipmunklike cheeks proved full and rosy. He looked healthy and happy, a child well tended and well loved.

Michael turned to Heather and caught her anxious

gestures, the sharp intake of breath, the tightly clasped hands.

Were they doing the right thing? Michael's phones, including his office line, had indeed been bugged, and Sims and Hoyt were truly FBI. Which, at the moment, seemed like an oxymoron. The mob and the government.

Whom were they supposed to trust?

Denny Halloway or Big Brother?

Michael entered the driveway, then halted before he reached the intercom. "Do you think Halloway knows about Sims and Hoyt? That they came to see us?"

"It's possible." Heather reached for her purse and placed it on her lap. She'd dressed western today— jeans, cowboy boots, a white T-shirt with a colorful row of seed beads decorating the collar.

"And what about Sims and Hoyt? Do you think they know we're here?"

"Probably."

Was everybody watching everybody, waiting to see who would crack first?

Michael rolled down the window and stopped at the intercom, announcing their arrival.

A disembodied voice gave them permission to enter just as an electronic gate creaked open.

The driveway wound into a semicircle, ending in front of the house. Or the mansion, Michael supposed. It was certainly big enough to claim that kind of grandeur.

Heather didn't react, but she'd been here before, the day she'd returned Beverly to her family.

He parked behind a black Mercedes. "Did Halloway pay attention to Justin last time?"

"Not really. He was engrossed in his daughter. In discovering she was ill."

"How's Beverly's mother handling all of this?" he asked, realizing she'd never mentioned Halloway's wife.

"She died a long time ago."

And now the mobster's daughter was dying, as well. Punishment for his sins? Or had life simply dealt him the death card?

"He has mistresses," she said. "Women Beverly never cared for."

He looked up and saw a dark-suited man at the front door. "Is that our Mafia king?"

Heather shook her head. "No. That's not him."

But either way, criminals beckoned. The West Cost Family. The Hollywood Mob. Michael couldn't have imagined this in a thousand years.

What in the hell had Reed been thinking? A Cherokee boy from the Hill Country had no business hobnobbing with big city killers.

Heather exited the SUV and unbuckled Justin from his car seat. Michael locked gazes with the wide-shouldered man at the door.

He wasn't a butler or manservant. This big, burly dude was a bodyguard.

Justin went willingly into Heather's arms, but a moment later he reached out to Michael.

"He wants his daddy," she said, her voice not quite steady.

"Come on, buddy." He took the child and brushed the baby's cheek with a kiss. Justin made a smacking noise and patted Michael's face. Heather moved beside him, preparing to ascend the brick steps.

The bodyguard had a prizefighter's face, tough and

gnarled. He had a boxer's fists, too. Hands the size
of two holiday-baked hams.

"You look like you're related to Blackwood," the
giant said to Michael. "More than she does." He
cocked his chin at Heather, who appeared much too
fragile with her fair skin and white-blond hair.

"I guess it's the Cherokee thing." How many
times had this guy's nose been broken? Michael
wouldn't have minded taking a pop at it himself.

They followed him into the house, stopping in the
foyer when he did. Another bodyguard appeared,
making the luxurious mansion seem like a fortress.

The first one, the boxer, rounded on Michael.
"Cute kid. You packin'?"

Caught off guard, he shifted the baby. "What?
No."

"Mind if I check?"

Hell, yes, he minded. But he knew he had little
choice. He transferred Justin into Heather's arms and
held up his hands, surrendering to the mob, to the
bastards that had eavesdropped on his life.

The search was quick, yet thorough. When the
boxer gazed at Heather, Michael snarled.

"If you so much as try to frisk her, I'll jam my fist
straight down your throat."

The giant chuckled. "You even act like Blackwood. Big in the balls department." The amused expression disappeared. "Too bad he screwed up." He
gazed at Heather again. "I used to like your brother."

She released a tight breath. "I still like him."

"Yeah. Family is family. Unless they stab you in
the back."

Which Reed had apparently done to the mob, Michael thought, wondering how long his old friend would survive this mess.

The boxer led them past a sweeping staircase and into a dark, masculine office. Gesturing for them to sit, he stood to the side of an ornate desk, his beefy arms at his sides. The second bodyguard waited, as well.

The boss arrived. Medium-boned, with grayish-blond hair and a well-tailored suit, he entered the room like a corporate mogul.

He said "Good afternoon," to Heather and offered Michael a proper handshake.

He wasn't what Michael expected. He didn't strut his stuff like the late John Gotti, the cocky New York mobster who reigned in most people's minds. Nor did he mumble through cotton padding in his mouth, the way Marlon Brando had done in his rendition of a Mafia Don. Halloway simply carried himself like any other successful Los Angeles businessman. But snakes came in all shapes and sizes, and in spite of his La-La Land breeding, Michael was certain Halloway slithered more often than not.

Nonetheless, he accepted the proffered hand.

"I'm pleased you're on time," Halloway said.

"You bugged my phones," Michael responded, just as politely, throwing the pretentious mobster a Texas curveball.

"Did we?" The boss blinked, almost smiled. "I don't recall doing such a thing." He glanced at the boxer. "Do you?"

The big man shrugged. "Maybe Blackwood did it. He's the surveillance expert, not me."

Halloway's features hardened. "My daughter's dying. Blackwood practically sent her back to me in a box.''

Suddenly Michael didn't know what to say, so he remained quiet, watching Reed's enemy walk toward Heather.

''You have a handsome son.'' He cast a look over his shoulder, shooting his words at Michael. ''I have three sons. But only one daughter.''

''When can I see Beverly?'' Heather asked, holding Justin close.

''Soon.'' Halloway continued to study the child, and Michael's heart nearly burst out of his chest. Did the mobster know? Did he know Justin was his grandson? His daughter's little boy?

Finally he turned back to Michael. ''The next time you see Blackwood, tell him that I reserved a room for him in hell.''

''I don't plan on seeing him. We're not friends anymore.''

''One never knows.'' The boss gestured to the boxer. ''Show the lady and her Indian lover upstairs.''

With that, he came around to his desk, dismissing them like last week's trash.

But Michael refused to let it end, not like that. ''Can I trust you, Halloway? Or is my family in danger?''

One graying eyebrow lifted. ''I don't prey on women and children.'' He reached into a humidor for a cigar, slid it beneath his nose. ''As for you.'' He paused, drew out his words for effect. ''I used to admire the Native American culture before Blackwood tainted my view. So quite frankly, Elk, your lack of respect is grating on me.''

Heather reached for Michael's arm, drawing him

away from the confrontation, and he saw the tremor in her eyes, the warning to keep his mouth shut.

They followed the boxer toward the elegant staircase, their boots sounding on a black-and-white display of expensive tile. At the top of the stairs, a suite-size bedroom presented impressive antiques, an around-the-clock nurse and a feeble young woman lost in a canopied bed.

Justin made a distressed sound, then arched toward his biological mother, squirming uncomfortably in Heather's arms. She moved forward, and the boxer took up residence in a conspicuous spot near the window, his big, broad frame flooded with sunlight.

The uniformed nurse, who kept vigil in a padded chair, glanced up from her book.

Heather sat on the edge of the bed, bringing Justin closer to his mom.

Michael held back, studying Beverly with a troubled heart. Pale and weak, she had honey-colored hair and soft green eyes, wise and sad beyond her years. An oxygen tank stood nearby, providing the breath of life. An IV dripped fluids and painkillers through her veins.

"Pa...pa...pa." Justin dropped his pony onto the bed, offering it to Beverly. Asking, Michael presumed, for her to turn the key, to play his favorite music.

Beverly's weary fingers crept toward it, and he knew Heather was blinking back tears.

Michael shifted his gaze to the boxer, wondering if he would react, but the burly man remained stoic. The nurse remained expressionless, as well.

No one suspected who Justin was, that the little boy

was the heir to Denny Halloway's crime-infested empire.

Because Beverly couldn't quite manage the toy, Heather helped her. When the lullaby drifted through the sterile room, Justin leaned against his new mom and watched his old one with big, dark eyes.

Torn with emotion, Michael thought about Reed, about the loss of his woman, the loss of his child.

And suddenly he was afraid.

Of losing everything that mattered to him, too.

The hotel room on Wilshire Boulevard was quiet. Images flickered on the TV screen, but the volume remained on Mute. Housekeeping had provided a crib for Justin, and Heather stood beside it, watching the baby sleep.

Michael sat on the edge of the bed, the remnants of room-service meals on the table next to him. He scrubbed his hand across his face, wondering what to say to Heather. So many thoughts spilled in and out of his mind, so many emotions he tried to contain.

"Beverly was so frail," Heather said, her voice quavering. She turned, looked at him. "Do you think Justin understands what's going on? Do you think he knows she's dying?"

Unsure of how to comfort her, he released a ragged breath. "He's too young to know. Children don't understand death. Especially babies."

"You're right. I'm just—"

Lost and grieving, he thought. "I'm sorry. I know how difficult this is for you."

She sighed, came toward him. She hadn't cried yet, but he sensed she would. Sooner or later, her tears would flow. "Thank you for being here, Michael. For being with me."

Heather sat beside him, and their shoulders brushed. They were both dressed for bed. He wore boxers, and she wore a soft, shimmering nightgown.

A lump formed in his throat. "I thought about Reed today. About what he's losing."

Her eyes turned watery. "There's nothing left for him."

"He has you. He knows you'll take care of his son." And that had been weighing on his mind all day. Reed had given Justin to Heather. But he'd given the child to Michael, as well.

She rose and reached for her water. Standing in front of the window, she took a small sip.

Behind her, the City of Angels embraced the night. Streetlamps illuminated well-traveled roads, and neon signs blazed. Overpasses crossed freeways, the glare from headlights spinning like pinwheels.

"Did you mean what you said earlier?" she asked.

"What did I say?"

"That Justin and I are your family." She paused, still clutching her water. "You asked Halloway if your family was safe. Me and Justin."

He squeezed his eyes shut, blocking out the city glare. Then he opened them and studied Heather, focusing on the woman who'd left him, the woman who'd returned with a baby who wasn't his.

"You feel like family. You've been in my life since I was a boy. And I'm—" He stalled, glanced at the crib. The baby slept soundly, snuggled beneath a white blanket. "Getting attached to Justin."

"I still love you, Michael."

Oh, God. Those familiar words ghosted through

him. He couldn't repeat them. He couldn't let himself go that far, feel that deeply.

"I want to make this work," he said instead. "I'm willing to try."

Her eyes were still watery. "This? You mean us?"

He nodded. He could see that he'd wounded her. That not telling her what she'd hoped to hear deflated her heart. "I worry about losing you. About you going away and not coming back. For good next time."

She set her glass on the table. "I won't leave."

"But you will. If we can't make it work, you'll go." What else could he offer but honesty? The rational way he looked at life? "When you disappeared, when I'd learned that you'd purposely deceived me, it was as if my worst nightmare had come true." He met her gaze, noticed the brilliant color of her irises. "I tried to go on. And I did, for the most part." He'd gone to work every day, kept in touch with friends, stayed close to his uncle. "But in some ways, I didn't. I didn't allow another woman into my bed."

She moved forward. "I'm glad you didn't."

"I was hoping you'd come back. Praying that you would. Praying and cursing and drinking. It wasn't healthy." He reached a hand out, drawing her closer. "I don't want you and Justin to leave next month. I want you to stay."

Her fingertips touched his. "I want that, too."

"But you want more. More than I'm capable of."

"You've been hurt. It'll take time."

Michael frowned. Who was she trying to convince? Him? Her? Both if them? "Falling in love scares me."

Her eyes widened. "You've never said that before. You've never admitted…" Her voice trailed.

Was she stunned? Disappointed? Hopeful? He couldn't be sure. "I saw what it did to my mom. She lived her entire life missing my father. A man who broke her heart."

Heather chewed her lip. "You're afraid I'll hurt you again?"

He continued to hold her gaze. "Can you honestly promise that you won't?"

She blinked, her lashes sweeping her cheeks. "I can try."

Clever answer, he thought. Clever, beautiful girl. But vulnerable, too. She looked like an angel, a celestial being struggling with the darkness in the world. The need for attachment. The torture of death.

"I'm sorry," he said. "I shouldn't have brought this up. Beverly probably won't make it through the week, and Reed is out there, alone somewhere. You have enough to contend with."

"Don't be sorry. Not now. Not when you just asked me to stay."

She slid into his embrace, and he knew she was going to cry. The dam had broken, the flood released.

He lifted her onto his lap, and she clung to him, her arms draped around his neck. Her tears fell silently, but he felt them on his shoulder, dampening his skin.

A part of him wished he could love her, that he could free the demon. The man who'd fallen apart when she'd left. The man who'd drunk himself into quiet stupors.

But he couldn't, so he simply comforted her, offering solace on a grief-ravaged night.

Stroking her hair, he brought her closer. Her breath

caught, her heartbeat thudded against his. Then her nightgown shimmied against his body, silk to skin.

She drew back, looked into his eyes. "Touch me, Michael."

She needed him, he realized. Needed to feel his hands molding her, arousing her, making her forget that her friend was dying, that her brother had been marked for a hit.

He needed that, too. The soft, liquid flow of love-making.

Michael turned off the lights, eased her onto the bed and kissed her. Tonight, he would be gentle, as tender as a big, broad-shouldered man could be. She seemed small beneath him, lean and lithe and fragile.

She arched and sighed, stretching her body in a catlike motion. He caressed her through the night-gown, thumbing her nipples, rubbing them into sensitive peaks. Then he lowered his head and sucked one into his mouth, leaving a warm, wet spot on the silk.

The mute television still flickered, and lights still blanketed the city, like wish-enhanced stars. Justin slept on the other side of the room, lost in lullaby ponies and fairy-tale dreams.

Knights and ladies, Michael thought. Dragon slay-ers and ancient seas. He'd dreamed when he was a boy, too. But now he was a man with a beautiful woman sweet and pliant beneath him.

He played her, like fingers skimming piano keys. Lowering the straps on her nightgown, he slid the garment from her body, watched it hug her curves until it pooled in his hands.

Her panties were a wisp of cotton and lace. He peeled them down, and she lifted her hips.

Without words, without promises, he gave her what she wanted, what she needed, kissing between her legs, making her rub against his mouth.

"Michael." She whispered his name, slid her fingers through his hair.

Slowly, deliberately, he brought her to a sweet, syrupy orgasm. Warm and wet against his tongue, her flavor filled his senses.

He rose above her, tugged off his boxers and sank into her, moving in a lover's dance.

This was their fairy tale, he thought. Their moment to lust, to linger, to drift on an ancient sea. They joined hands, fingers entwined, and a smooth, sensual current flowed between them.

The reality of making love on the wings of a dream.

Nine

Two days after Heather and Michael returned to Texas, they took Justin to the barn, determined to introduce him to the horses on the ranch.

Life was somehow settled yet confusing, Heather thought, as they strode along a row of box stalls. Michael had asked her to stay, to live with him again. But even so, he hadn't made a commitment.

Would he ever? Or was that a hope? A pipedream? A coin-in-the-fountain wish that would never come true?

She glanced at her lover, saw the paternal look in his eyes. Justin rode in his arms, pampered and content.

"This is Sir Caballero," Michael told the baby, stopping in front of a gelding's stall. "Sir Knight. He's one of our favorites."

"Ooooh." Wide eyed, Justin stared at the horse.

"You can pet him. Like this." He took the child's hand and guided it along Caballero's nose.

The gelding nickered, and Justin gasped.

Michael chuckled. "That's just horse talk. He's greeting you." He turned to Heather. "I need to teach this little guy to ride."

She couldn't help but smile. "He's still a bit young."

He shrugged, grinned. "When he's older."

Her heart went soft, melting in her chest. Little by little, Michael was becoming Justin's father. He was even contemplating the future, planning father-son activities in his mind.

"Ba…ba…ba. Pa…pa…pa." Justin chattered, and the gelding perked his ears.

"See. He's listening to you," Michael explained. "When a horse is relaxed and his ears are forward, he's expressing interest. Now, when he pins his ears, he's pissed. I mean angry." He caught himself, slanted Heather a sheepish grin and continued, "You don't want to pet a horse when he's angry. Isn't that right, Mommy?"

"Yes." A sense of family winged through her, a flutter of belonging, of wishes coming true.

Justin babbled again, and Heather studied Michael's profile, the slant of his cheekbone, the cut of his jaw. Did Justin truly resemble him? Or did people only see what they expected to see?

Michael Elk's son.

Suddenly her stomach tensed.

He had a right to know about the other baby. The child she'd borne, the infant who'd died. But she couldn't tell him. Not now. Their reconciliation was too new, too fragile. What if he blamed her for their baby's death?

Heather's mouth went dry. When should she tell him? Six months from now? A year? How much time would pass before their relationship solidified? Before the secret she'd been keeping wouldn't shatter his soul?

He was afraid to love her, afraid she would hurt him.

What about forgiveness? Was he capable of absolving her? Or were her sins too grave? She'd left without telling him she was pregnant; she'd returned without telling him his son had died.

The baby who'd been buried without a headstone, without a name.

The other pony.

Michael's voice sliced into her thoughts.

"Let's go outside," he said to Justin, who wiggled in his arms. "We can watch Uncle Bobby work."

Heather told herself to stay strong, to thank God for giving her a second chance with the man she loved. She couldn't turn back the clock, but she could move forward, be a loyal mate, a caring mother.

"Maybe we can picnic later," she said. "Order something from the chef."

Michael smiled. "Sounds good to me. How about you, buddy?"

Justin grinned his approval, and they exited the barn and made contact with the spring air.

The ranch presented sights and sounds from nature. The hills, formed from a limestone bedrock, rose in the distance, and a mild breeze blew, rattling leaves on trees. A floral aroma blended with hay, horses and grass.

In a nearby arena, Bobby coached his student, a young man urging his mount into a fluid lope.

Chester fit into the scene, too. The mutt lolled in the shade, yawning big and wide.

Michael stopped to greet his pet. "What are you doing, Ches?"

Heather eyed the dog. "A whole lot of nothing, from the look of him. Mr. Lazy Bones."

"Da...da...da," Justin said, chiming into the conversation.

"Does that mean Daddy?" Michael asked.

"Actually—" she paused, met the anticipation in his eyes "—it means dog."

"Oh." His voice fell.

"But it could mean Daddy, too." She moved closer, needing to keep the family connection alive.

"Daddy-Dog, huh?" He chuckled. "I think I'll pass that one along to Reed."

"*Michael.*" With a playful scold, she bumped his arm.

His expression turned serious. "He's going to be calling soon, isn't he?"

"Yes." She knew he'd begun to worry about her brother, to think of him with compassion. "It'll be good to hear his voice."

They headed to the arena, stood at the fence rail.

Justin watched the man on horseback, and Heather recalled lighter-hearted days. Mornings when she, Reed and Michael used to trail ride in the hills.

"I'm glad you're going to teach Justin to ride someday," she said.

"Yeah. All Native babies should be cowboys."

"Or cowgirls," she put in.

He nodded, and they remained outdoors, letting the

day slip by comfortably. They walked in the sun, relaxed in the shade, tossed a Frisbee with Chester and picnicked on a bench near the chef's garden.

Hours later, they returned to the farmhouse, a sleepy Justin in tow. Heather put him down for a nap and joined Michael in the living room.

He stood beside the desk, the phone to his ear, checking voice mail messages. Then his expression darkened.

"What is it?" she asked.

"It was Halloway." His cleared his throat, gave her a troubled look. "Beverly died this morning."

Heather drew a choppy breath. She'd known this was coming, but it still hurt, still lanced her like an arrow.

Uneasy, he shuffled some papers on the rolltop desk. "The funeral is on Tuesday. Halloway said we're not welcome. He doesn't want us there."

A flood of tears rushed her eyes. Beverly was truly gone. There were no more goodbyes.

And then another thought filtered through her mind, wrapping itself around her heart.

Beverly was with the other pony now, watching over the child Heather had lost.

Michael's son.

Clinging to the comfort of heaven, she moved to stand beside him.

In the silence that followed, in the fading light of dusk, he reached for her. She put her head on his shoulder and promised herself that she would tell him about their baby.

Someday. When the time was right.

The day had come. Heather waited by the scrambler-activated phone, anxious for her brother to call.

Michael sat on the sofa, turning pages in a pop-up book for Justin. The baby cuddled on his lap, watching the three-dimensional pictures come to life.

"Wa?" the child said in an inquisitive tone.

"That's a tiger." Michael struck a ferocious pose. *"Grrr."*

"Grrr." Justin mimicked him, right down to both hands poised in the air like claws.

Heather gazed at the boy, at his funny little snarling expression. She knew Michael was keeping Justin entertained until she heard from Reed.

"What if he doesn't call?" she said suddenly.

"He will."

"But what if he doesn't?"

Her question hung in the air. If her brother didn't call, then he was in trouble. Possibly even dead. The mob hadn't given up. A hired gun was still on the case, a hit man whose sole purpose was to hunt down Beverly's old lover and kill him.

"I can't help but worry," she said.

Michael glanced at the clock, turned another page for Justin. "He's not due to call just yet."

No, there were still twenty minutes to spare.

She blew out a breath and told herself to relax. Surely, Reed would continue to outfox the mob.

Wouldn't he?

Her brother was a genius, smarter than some money-grubbing hit man.

She adjusted her chair at the desk and thanked God for Michael and the baby. Her family. Her support group.

Justin pointed to another figure popping out of the book. "Wa?"

"That's a giraffe." Michael stalled, searching for a noise to describe the animal. Then he stretched his neck, using a visual aid instead. "They're tall. See? They touch the top of the trees."

Justin craned his neck, too.

"That's right." Pride sounded in his voice. "We've got a smart kid here."

Smart. "Like my brother."

"Yes, like your brother." Thoughtful, Michael smoothed the baby's hair. "Why did Halloway forbid Reed from dating Beverly?"

"Because there are rules to follow. Rules the mob enforces. Engaging in an affair with the wife, daughter or sister of another member is prohibited. Punishable by death."

"But Reed wasn't playing around. He wanted to marry Beverly. Is there a rule against that?"

"Not if permission is granted, but some mobsters don't want their daughters marrying men from their organization. They don't even want their sons involved."

"Yeah, but Halloway isn't like that. Aren't his sons prominent members of the West Coast Family?"

She nodded. "Halloway promotes them. His oldest is his underboss."

"Then why not promote the man who was in love with his daughter? Who wanted to marry her? Why beat the crap out of Reed and warn him to stay away from Beverly?"

"Most men are protective of their daughters, even men like Halloway."

"I think there's more to it than that."

"Reed and Beverly never mentioned anything."

"Maybe it was something they didn't want you to

know.'' Michael turned the next page, and Justin studied a python, its coiled body arched to strike. "I'll bet the FBI knows. I'll bet they know exactly what went on.''

She reached for the card Sims had given them. She kept it handy, prepared to give Reed the information.

"Wa?" Justin asked, still engaged in the book.

"Snake," Michael told him. "Like Denny Halloway.''

Fifteen minutes passed. Then thirty.

Heather watched the clock, focusing on every second that Reed was late. Maybe he wasn't as smart as she'd given him credit for. Maybe he'd gotten tripped up.

Michael put the baby on the floor. Justin had grown tired of jungle creatures and wanted to lie on a pillow with Chester.

"Da...da...da," he said, patting the pooch. Chester gave the boy a big, sloppy kiss but Heather couldn't find the strength to smile.

Beverly had been buried yesterday, and Reed—

The telephone rang, screeching like a siren.

She grabbed the receiver, felt her heart pound. "Hello?"

"I'm sorry I'm late," a familiar voice said.

She sighed and nodded to Michael, who watched her, waiting for confirmation that the person on the other end of the line was her brother.

She scooted in her chair, holding the phone close to her ear. "I've been so worried."

"I thought I was being followed. It turned out to be nothing.''

Heather's throat tightened. Should she tell him about Beverly? Tell him she was dead?

"How's it going with you and Michael?" he asked.

"We're getting closer every day." Closer, she prayed, to a commitment. "He's a good father. As good as you said he would be."

A pause, then an emotional, "How's Justin?"

She glanced at the baby. He chewed on a teething ring while Chester gnawed on a bone. "He's perfect. Healthy and happy. He loves the ranch."

"I miss him."

"I know." She also knew this conversation would be short, even if it was encrypted. Reed didn't take chances, not anymore. "The FBI was here."

"Why? What did they want?"

"They said they might be able to help." She picked up Sims' card. "They left their names and number. Write it down, okay?"

"Are you sure they're FBI?"

"Yes. Michael checked them out." She read the information on the card, knew he was scratching it out in his Einstein script.

"Are you going to call them?" she asked.

"I don't know. I have to think about it."

"I want you to be safe." She pictured him, with his broad shoulders and hard, angular face. He looked as tough as he was. "I love you."

"I love you, too."

Such easy words, she thought. Easy between siblings. She glanced at Michael. Difficult between lovers.

His voice broke. "Give Justin a kiss from me. Hold him, show him how much I care."

Her eyes filled with tears. She couldn't do it. She couldn't tell her brother that Beverly was dead.

"I'll try to call again. But I can't be sure when," he said.

"I'll be prepared." She would keep the scrambler ready, keep this line open for his calls.

"Thank Michael for me. Tell him…" A gruff pause, a cleared throat. "Just say thanks."

"I will."

"Bye, Blondie Bear." He used the nickname he'd given her when they were children. "And don't forget that kiss, that hug for Justin."

"I won't. I promise I won't."

A second later, the line went dead, leaving nothingness in her ear.

Michael picked up the baby and came toward her. "Is he all right?"

"He sounded lonely. Distant. Like he was trying to keep himself from feeling too much." She placed the phone on its cradle and reached for Justin, holding him close, pressing her lips to his cheek. A kiss from Reed, from the daddy he'd lost. "I couldn't bring myself to tell him about Beverly."

"I don't blame you." He jammed his hands into his pockets, frowned a little.

They remained silent for a moment, both thinking about Beverly, recalling her on her deathbed.

"Why do you think she fell for Reed?" Michael asked. "If she detested her father's business, then what made Reed, one of her dad's soldiers, so appealing?"

Heather sighed. "People can't help who they fall in love with."

His frown deepened, and she quelled the pain of not being loved, of hoping and dreaming. He didn't understand what Reed and Beverly had, the consuming need to be together, to get married, to raise a family, to share every aspect of their lives.

"I'm sorry," he said. "I didn't mean to imply that Reed wasn't worthy of Beverly."

"Reed used to say the same thing. That he wasn't good enough for her."

He smoothed a strand of her hair, comforting her, trying to dissolve the melancholy, to let it drift away. "Are you hungry? I can fix dinner."

He must have known that she hadn't eaten, except for a few sparse bites at breakfast. "What are you going to make?"

"Whatever you're in the mood for."

"You decide." Anything was fine, anything that would revive her weary system.

She followed him into the kitchen, sat on a nearby stool and watched the culinary preparation. After he marinated chicken breasts, he popped them in the oven, along with diced carrots and rosemary-seasoned potatoes.

While the food filled the old farmhouse with a tasty aroma, he removed a box of instant pudding and dumped the contents into a bowl.

Milk was added, and the electric mixer sounded, whipping the vanilla concoction into a thick swirl.

Justin crooned "Um…um…um," and they both laughed.

Michael reached for a spoon. "Somebody wants dessert."

As he scooped some pudding into a plastic bowl for the baby, she said, "Reed told me to thank you."

"Really?" He looked up and smiled. "I think it's working. Us being parents."

"Me, too." She brought Justin to his new daddy.

And when the three of them embraced, she let the feeling, the simple of joy of having a family, sweep her away.

The Corral, the local honky-tonk, boasted scarred oak walls, live country music and pool tables near the backdoor. Sawdust littered the floor, and rustic table-tops provided fat white candles and bowls of peanuts.

Michael and Heather occupied a cozy spot near a window. This was a date, a night on the town he'd arranged. He wasn't sure if Heather considered a few hours at the Corral romantic, but he did. The band that utilized the stage was known for slow, crooning ballads. Michael intended to dance, to show the local patrons that his lady was back, that he wasn't sitting at a bar stool by himself, staring into space and nursing a mind-numbing beer.

"I'm a little nervous," Heather said.

"Why? What's wrong?"

"This is the first time I've left Justin alone."

"He's not alone. He's with Bobby and Julianne." They'd sent Chester along, too. And of course baby Brendan was there, as well. "He's in good hands."

She sighed. "I know, but…"

"Here." He handed her his cell phone. "Call them. Find out how he's doing." He didn't want her worrying. He hoped for a relaxing evening, a night away from the turmoil in their lives. He knew she was still mourning Beverly, still fretting about her brother's safety.

She dialed the number and waited for someone to answer. Michael sipped his soda. He'd decided not to drink tonight, not to blur his brain with alcohol. He'd done enough of that to last a lifetime.

''Hi. Julianne? It's Heather. I was wondering how Justin is doing.'' She sat a little straighter, listened to the voice on the other end of the line. ''Really? I'm so glad. Yes, please, put him on.'' Covering the mouthpiece, she looked up at Michael. ''Justin is coming to the phone.''

He shot her an amused grin. The kid was going to babble a bunch of nonsense, the way he did on his toy phone.

''Hi, sweetie,'' she said, her tone softening. ''Are you having fun?''

Michael watched her expression, the maternal glow in her eyes. She simply sat, a smile on her face, listening to Justin prattle.

After a short while, she said, ''I love you. Kiss Chester goodnight for me, and Daddy and I will see you later.'' She spoke to Julianne again, then ended the call.

''Feel better?'' he asked.

''Much.'' She returned his phone. ''Julianne said Bobby's been giving Justin piggyback rides.''

''Really?'' Michael hadn't thought of entertaining Justin in that manner, but this daddy stuff was still a bit new.

New, but cool. He liked being a father.

Heather met his gaze, and he studied her, the way her hair framed her face, the glow of her candlelit skin.

He'd always been fascinated by her, even when they were kids, when her chest was flat and her knees were knobby.

''You were cute when you were young,'' he said.

She picked up her wine, took a sip. ''Cute?''

"I liked that you had a crush on me. It made me feel important."

"You were important. The only boy I wanted to be with. Of course, there was that hunk who took me to the prom. He was a pretty good kisser. And he—"

"Knock it off." He all but snapped out the words, springing them like rubber bands. He recalled her prom date, recalled how proper and gentlemanly the guy was, just the type Heather should have ended up with, the stable, fall-in-love sort Michael could never be.

She toyed with her cocktail napkin, gave him a coy smile. "Jealous?"

"Damn right." He flicked a peanut at her and made her laugh.

"As if you didn't put me through the wringer. So I kissed a few boys. How many women have you been with?"

He shrugged, spun the ice in his glass. "Can I help it if I'm so irresistible?"

She narrowed her pretty eyes at him. "They were bimbos, Michael. Hardly worth bragging about."

And he'd slept with most of them during a time when she'd been forbidden to him. "I was waiting for you."

"By bedding every blonde in town? That's quite a sacrifice."

Michael cursed his stupidity. He hadn't brought her here to joke about the past, to make wisecracks that cut bone deep.

"Do you want to dance?" he asked.

Her gaze met his, and she seemed to relax, to appreciate the shift of topic, the suggestion to hold each other.

The song was easy, the mood light and sensual. Heather's body fit perfectly against his, her long, lean curves pressing intimately.

He lowered his head to kiss her, tasting her warmth, her sweetness, the wine flavoring her lips. Afterward, she looked into his eyes, dazzling him, making every nerve ending under his skin come alive.

"I love you, Michael."

Breathless, he nearly stumbled. "You shouldn't say that."

"I can't help it."

And neither could he. He wouldn't allow himself to love her, but that didn't stop the obsession, the need, the desperation of wanting her.

"Just don't leave me again," he said.

"I won't."

"Promise?"

"Yes."

She brushed her lips against his cheek, and he prayed he wasn't fooling himself. That he wouldn't wake up one night and discover she was gone.

Ten

Three days passed, with spring edging closer to summer, with warm, dry winds billowing through open windows.

Awakening in the dark, Michael rolled over and reached for Heather. Stretching his arm farther, he connected with her pillow.

And discovered she wasn't there.

Panicked, he shot out of bed and grabbed his jeans, blinking and squinting at the clock on the dresser: 4:05. The moon was still out.

He checked the bathroom first, then the nursery. The baby slept, but Heather was nowhere to be found.

Even though he knew she wouldn't leave Justin behind, he couldn't stop the flash of fear slamming through his veins. What if the mob took her? What if Halloway had lied about not preying on women?

He dashed into the living room, noticed the porch light and released a shaky breath.

Much too anxious, he swung open the front door. She sat on the swing, a silky robe belted over her nightgown. "Damn it, Heather. You scared me. I didn't know where the hell you were."

Her hand flew to her heart, and he realized his harsh tone had startled her.

In spite of her jumpiness, she looked beautiful, soft and delicate in the amber light, with the vast Texas sky and the night-shadowed hills framed like a photo behind her.

"I was going to get you up soon," she said.

"Why?"

"Reed called."

His pulse pounded. "When?"

"The phone woke me about an hour ago. He wants us to meet him. After the sun comes up. In the smoking cave."

Her brother was here, in Texas? "What's going on?"

"I don't know. He didn't give me much to go on. He said to make sure there's no one following us. And to bring Justin."

"On that trail?" The narrow path to the smoking cave, to the secret place where Reed and Michael used to share cigarettes, was only accessible by foot. "How are we supposed to haul Justin up that hill?"

She rocked the swing, her voice quiet yet determined. "I have a baby carrier Reed used to cart Justin around in. It's like a backpack. We can use that."

He frowned, worried where this was leading. "I don't understand what your brother is up to. Why take a chance like this? Why come to Texas?"

"He said it's important. Really important. I think it has something to do with the FBI."

Michael quit arguing. He could see that Heather intended to meet with Reed, to bring the baby, with or without him. And no damn way would he let her go alone.

They showered and dressed, then got Justin ready.

The drive to the hills proved quiet. The sun broke through the clouds, sending a reddish-gold hue across the sky. The baby drank his bottle in the back seat, unaware and unfazed by the early-morning outing.

Michael took the winding road as far as he could and parked at a lookout point near a ledge. Heather helped him settle Justin into the baby carrier on his back, and they hiked the rest of the way.

The limestone-based soil supported cedar and live oak, and the narrow path wound past trees and spiny brush. The sight of the cave, partially hidden by branches, brought back childhood memories, images of two wild-spirited boys, testing the boundaries of youth.

Michael and Heather entered the cave and stood near the opening, where a small amount of light trickled in.

Soon a tall, dark figure emerged.

"Reed." Heather whispered her brother's name and moved forward, hugging him.

When she stepped back, Michael noticed the changes in the other man. His hard-edged face was leaner, and his long dark hair had been shorn. He wore a cowboy hat dipped low on his forehead, the brim shading his eyes.

His body was leaner, too. But still corded with

muscle. He looked haunted. And dangerous. Every bit the desperado he was.

Heather removed Justin from the baby carrier, and when the boy spotted his father, he gasped and reached out, anxious to make contact.

Justin hadn't reacted this strongly to Beverly, but she had been confined to a bed, with tubes attached to her body.

Reed took his son, holding him close.

Michael felt a pang of envy. Then a stab of fear. Did the other man intend to resume custody? To take away the child Michael had agreed to claim?

"Sims and Hoyt are waiting for me at the campground," Reed said. "I don't have much time."

Heather gazed at her brother. "They're helping you?"

"Yes." He kissed Justin, allowing the affection to linger. "They're offering me protection for my testimony. There was a murder Halloway orchestrated, and I—" He paused, drew a breath. "I was there. I knew it was going to happen."

Had Reed been implicated in the crime? Michael wondered. Was the FBI granting him immunity?

"The mob was testing me," Reed said, as if he'd read Michael's mind. "I didn't fail, but I didn't pass, either. At the time, they weren't sure if the mistake I'd made was deliberate or not."

"What mistake?" Michael asked, trapping Heather's brother with a frown.

"I was supposed to cause a distraction so the hit could go down. And I did, but not the way I'd been instructed to do. I was trying to prevent it. But it didn't work. I couldn't stop it."

And that was something Reed would always detest

himself for, Michael thought. Heather's brother was a thief, but he wasn't a killer. Even though he'd known what the mob represented, he hadn't expected to watch someone die. Or God forbid, to be part of it.

Heather's breath rushed out. "You never told me any of this."

"I didn't tell Beverly, either. I didn't want either of you to know." Reed adjusted his son. "Once I enter the Witness Protection Program, they'll change my name, my face, my life history. It's supposed to help me start over. To quit running."

Michael stepped forward. "Are you taking Justin with you? Is that what this is all about?"

"No." Reed met his gaze, and for a moment, they simply stared at each other. Men who'd been friends; friends who'd become enemies. "I want to keep Justin, to raise him, to watch him grow up, but I can't." He rocked the child, making the little one sigh. "I didn't tell Sims and Hoyt that Justin is my son. I don't want anyone to know. Not even the feds. Sending Halloway to prison isn't enough. Beverly's brothers will still be out there. They'll still pose a threat. And if I take Justin with me, they'll figure it out. They'll know he's Beverly's boy." He shifted his stance, his time-worn boots making a pattern in the dirt. "Justin is better off with you and Heather. You can give him things I can only dream about, the happiness and security he deserves. He's your son," he said to Michael, his voice rough with emotion. "If you're willing to keep him."

"I am." Michael didn't stop to think about his response. It came quickly, naturally. He wanted Justin.

"I'll take good care of him. I'll be the best dad I can be."

"Thank you."

Reed transferred Justin into Michael arms, and he knew his old friend wanted to see them together, to reassure himself that he was doing the right thing.

Justin latched onto Michael's shirt and smiled at Reed. The boy's father smiled back, but his eyes were hazy, tearing in the misty light.

Heather cried, too. But unlike Reed, her tears flowed freely. She fell into her brother's embrace, and he held her, soothing her the way he'd done when they were children. From Michael's arms, Justin watched them, and he prayed the boy didn't reach for his father again, making this harder on Reed than it already was.

Heather stepped back and wiped her eyes, taking her brother's hands. "Beverly—"

He stopped her. "I know. She's gone." His voice turned rough again, his eyes still watery. "Sims and Hoyt told me. They also said that you and Michael went to see her. That you took Justin."

For a while no one spoke. Reed didn't ask about their trip to California, to provide details, for which Michael was grateful. The other man didn't need to hear how pale and weak Beverly had been, how small and frail she'd looked in that big, canopied bed, with a prim nurse and a burly bodyguard keeping watch.

Reed cleared his throat, breaking the silence. "The Witness Protection Program doesn't matter all that much to me. I'm indifferent about where I go. But I know it'll make you feel better." He gave his sister's chin a gentle cuff. "You won't have to worry about me anymore."

"Will I ever hear from you again?" she asked.

He touched her cheek, then looked at Justin, a look of longing, of loss. "No. This is the last time."

"Try to be happy," she told him, her voice quavering. "Try to make a new life for yourself."

He shrugged, but the gesture was strained, tight and uncomfortable. "It beats the mob catching up with me, I guess. And Sims and Hoyt aren't that bad."

"Hoyt's an ass," Michael put in, making Reed's stubborn lips quirk.

And then suddenly they were grinning at each other, like boyhood friends, like the Cherokee brothers they used to be.

This was goodbye, Michael thought. The end. Soon Reed Blackwood would become someone new. Reed extended his hand, but Michael embraced him instead, hugging Justin between them. The child laughed and squealed.

It was a joyous sound, a sound for Reed to cling to. He kissed Justin and told him that he loved him. He kissed Heather, too. And within seconds, he disappeared into the darkness of the cave, almost as if he'd never been there at all.

An uneventful week went by, and Michael enjoyed the easy pace. For the first time since Heather returned, he felt a sense of normalcy, a stream of pure contentment.

Was this what being married was like? he wondered, as he watched Heather smooth her dress. Was this the white-picket-fence dream other people worked so hard to achieve?

Seated on the edge of the bed, he caught her gaze in the armoire mirror. "You look nice, Heather."

"Thank you." She turned to face him. "Are you sure you're going to be okay by yourself?"

He rolled his eyes. "Hey, c'mon, I'm Justin's dad." And he'd offered to watch the baby while she attended a business meeting with the pain-in-the-ass bride. "You're probably going to have more trouble than I am. I feel sorry for that broad's fiancé."

Heather shook her head. "Broad?"

"Considering what I could've called her, I was being polite."

"I see." She pursed her lips. "Well, for your information, her fiancé is perfectly comfortable with their arrangement. He doesn't mind letting her be the boss."

Michael bounded off the bed. "'Cause he's a wuss."

"Unlike you?"

"Yeah, unlike me." Proving his point, he grabbed her shoulders and gave her a rough kiss.

When he released her, she teetered, a bit dizzy on her feet. Much too pleased with himself, he sent her a cocky grin.

"Oh, my." Lashes fluttering, she fanned her face and made him laugh.

"Wanna mess around later?" he asked, suddenly anxious for her to ditch the bitchy bride and return to his bed.

"I don't know. You might be too exhausted. After all, you've got a long day ahead of you. Bottles to wash, endless games of patty-cake and peekaboo to play, diapers to…" She tilted her head, measuring him. "Speaking of which, you still haven't changed a diaper. Are you sure you can handle this?"

"I'll be fine. Who can't wipe a kid's bottom and slap on a diaper?"

"Slap?"

"Tape, whatever. Those disposable things practically change themselves."

"Really?" Amused, she lifted her brows. "You mean I've been putting in too much effort all this time?"

"Very funny." He nudged her down the hall. "Just go. Conquer your meeting. Convince Miss Pain-in-the-Ass that she'll have the grandest wedding in Texas."

She started fretting. "Don't forget to give Justin his breakfast."

Did she think he would let the little one starve? "Just as soon as he wakes up, I'll fix him some oatmeal."

"He likes milk and honey in it."

"I know." He walked her to her car. She was headed to the city and needed to get going. "I'll call Julianne if I need anything. And if she's unavailable, I'll call Maria. There are plenty of kid-friendly women around here. You've got nothing to worry about."

"All right." She sighed, placed her briefcase on the passenger's seat. "Don't ply Justin with sweets. No banana cream pie."

"Spoilsport." He drew her against him. "How about some guacamole dip instead?"

"I guess that will be okay. But don't add anything to it but mayonnaise. Or a few mild spices." She gave him a prim kiss and shocked him silly when she pinched his butt.

They gazed at each other, laughed, then kissed for

real. A minute later, she disappeared down the road, leaving him standing in the driveway, looking after her.

Wondering if being married would be this cool.

He returned to the house, and Justin awakened quietly. Michael lifted him from the crib and placed him on the changing table.

"You don't smell too bad," he told the boy, grateful the diaper was merely wet.

Justin made a cranky face and rubbed his ears as if they itched.

"It's okay, buddy. I'll fix some oatmeal, and we can have some guacamole later." He poked the baby's belly but still no smile. "What's wrong? Do you miss your mom already? She'll be back before you know it."

He utilized the baby wipes, fit a fresh diaper into place and dumped the old one in a nearby pail. "We'll deal with a bath after breakfast."

Carting Justin into the kitchen, he told himself not to worry, even if the boy seemed distressed. A little food, a little playtime and everything would be all right.

Everything wasn't all right. Justin wouldn't eat. He sat in the high chair, whimpering, pushing Michael away whenever he brought the spoon near.

"I fixed it the way you like it. See?" He tasted the oatmeal himself.

Justin wasn't impressed. He rubbed his ears, the way he'd done earlier, and started to cry.

"Why don't we skip breakfast?" He removed the child from the high chair, then realized how warm Justin's skin was. "Are you sick? Is that the problem?"

Doing his damnedest to be a responsible dad, he located the thermometer, then wondered how he was supposed to keep it under the boy's tongue.

He gave up and called the doctor's office. Aware of his inexperience, the receptionist, a gal he'd gone to high school with, told him to take Justin's temperature under his arm and call her back.

Sure enough, the boy had a fever.

Ninety minutes later, Justin sat on the examining table in the doctor's office, making a pissy face at the kindly old physician.

"It's okay." Michael stroked the boy's back. "Just about everybody in town comes here when they're sick, including me. Dr. Mills knows what he's doing."

The gray-haired man chuckled. "You were a grumpy patient when you were a kid, too." Poking and prodding, he checked out the child. "Hmm." He flashed a light in Justin's ears, first one and then the other.

Michael knew instantly, recalling the ear rubbing the boy had done earlier. "He has an infection, doesn't he?"

"A mild one, but we'll take care of it." The doctor wrote a prescription for an antibiotic, adjusting his glasses as they slipped down his nose.

"I told his mom everything would be all right today."

"And it is. Your son is going to be just fine." Dr. Mills gazed at Michael for a moment, his tone a little deeper. "I'm glad Heather is back. I was worried about her."

"Yeah. Me, too."

"I knew she was pregnant, but I wasn't at liberty

to divulge that information then. I assumed it was your child, but after she disappeared, I didn't know what to think.''

Michael tried not to react, to lose his composure. ''Heather came to see you? Before she went to California?''

''She surely did. I gave her the result of the urinalysis myself.'' The doctor cupped Justin's cheek. ''And here's our proof. A handsome little Cherokee boy.''

''Yes.'' Michael lifted Justin and feigned a casual air, even though his heart, his betrayed heart, slammed against the wall of his chest.

If Heather had been pregnant, then where, dear God, was the baby?

Heather came home and found Michael slumped on the sofa, staring at the TV, flipping channels with the remote. He looked up at her, his eyes much too dark. Was he angry? Depressed? Tired?

''What's wrong?'' she asked.

''I took Justin to the doctor today.''

''Oh, my goodness, why?'' Fretful, she set her purse on the coffee table. ''Is he sick? Did he get hurt?''

''He has an ear infection. But the doctor said he'd be fine. I gave him his antibiotic and put him to bed.''

''I'm sorry you had to deal with that alone. I should have been here. I should have—''

''I had an interesting chat with Dr. Mills, Heather. You wouldn't believe what he told me.''

Oh, God.

His gaze drilled into hers, snaring her like a rabbit

caught in a trap. She wanted to run, skitter away, but she couldn't. So she stood, her limbs frozen.

He set the remote on Mute, shutting out the sound of the TV, leaving the room quiet.

Ghostly quiet.

She waited for the bomb to drop, for the past to explode in her face.

"Is it true?" he asked. "Were you pregnant when you left?"

A chill sliced her spine. He looked so hard, so unforgiving. His hair fell to his shoulders in a razor-sharp line, and shadows edged his face, leaving hollow marks beneath his cheekbones.

"Yes," she said. "It's true."

His mouth, set in a grim line, barely moved. The words that escaped his lips were tight and drawn. "What happened to the baby?"

Tears rose to her eyes. "He was stillborn."

Michael's voice turned raw. "He? We had a son?"

"Yes. He was born a week after Justin." Her mind slipped back to the pain, to the ache and confusion of losing a child. "It never occurred to me that anything could go wrong. Beverly was the one who struggled, who had a difficult pregnancy. I was healthy and strong."

"Then why did the baby die?"

"The umbilical cord got tangled. It—" She wrapped her arms around her body, hugging herself, consoling an ache that wouldn't heal. "Reed tried to save him, but he wasn't breathing."

She could still see herself, crying over the lifeless form. Her baby. Michael's child. "My brother buried him. He built a wood box and sprinkled it with sage."

Michael fell silent, and she wondered what he was

thinking, what he was feeling. Did he hate her now? Did he feel differently about Justin?

"What was his name?" he asked. "What was my son's name?"

"I never chose one. Reed said we should name our children the old Cherokee way, to wait until we saw them. Until they lived outside the womb." When her knees turned watery, she sat, sliding bonelessly into a nearby chair. "Before either baby was born, my brother brought home two stuffed ponies, one for his child and one for mine."

"The toy Justin likes so much," he said.

"Yes." She closed her eyes, opening them a moment later.

"What happened to the second pony?" he asked.

Weak with remembrance, she pressed a decorative pillow to her chest. "We buried it with the baby."

He turned toward the window, and she followed his gaze. The sun still blazed in the sky, sending golden streaks through the blinds.

"Where's his body?" He shifted to look at her. "I want to bring him home."

"You can't. Oh, God, Michael. You can't. If the mob finds out there was another child. If—"

"Damn you."

He cursed beneath his breath, and the words scraped her heart, like nails, broken and brittle, on a chalkboard.

"I'm sorry," she said. "I'm so sorry. It wasn't supposed to be like this."

"But it is, isn't it?"

He pulled a hand through his hair, and she knew he was craving a cigarette, keeping his hands busy to stop himself from trashing the house to find one. Finally he picked up a magazine and tossed it across the room. It landed against the wall, the pages spilling open.

She didn't flinch. She'd seen him do worse when he was hurt, when he crawled inside himself with the pain. He'd smashed a sink full of dishes when his mother had died. He'd cut his hands, then cried and bled. He'd been just a boy then, the boy Heather had always loved.

The man she kept hurting.

"Why didn't you tell me you were pregnant?" he asked. "Why did you go to California without telling me?"

She drew a breath, afraid of admitting the truth but knowing she had to. "I wanted to talk to Reed first. I knew you'd offer to marry me, and I was worried about it. Worried about marrying a man who didn't love me."

"People who have kids should be married."

"No, Michael. People should get married because they're in love. I didn't want you proposing for the wrong reason."

"And running off to see Reed was going to change that?"

"Reed thinks that you love me. He's thought that for years. And I wanted to hear him say it, to convince me it was true."

Silence stretched between them, a painful yawn in the golden light. What would happen when darkness fell? When the moon ghosted through the trees and the hills faded into the night?

Michael rose, the floorboards creaking beneath his boots. "I thought about it today. I wondered what it would be like to be married to you."

"You did?" Stunned, she rocked forward in her chair, her heart filling with hope, with a young, girlish prayer. "Why?"

"Because we were getting along so well. Because I was becoming Justin's dad. Because it felt right."

But not because he loved her, she realized.

Heather watched him walk out the door, where he stood on the porch and stared at the horizon. A tall, lone figure against the sun. The man she'd lost. The man she'd never really had.

Nothing had changed. With or without her betrayal, with or without their baby, Michael Elk didn't love her.

And he never would.

Eleven

Michael didn't try to sleep. Instead he roamed the house like a predator, drinking black coffee and dragging his hand through his hair. He wanted a cigarette so badly, he could scream, rage and tear down the walls.

But he refused to light up, to give in to temptation. One way or another, he would hold himself together.

Heather was in the guest room, tossing and turning, he suspected. She'd taken it upon herself to abandon him, to leave his bed empty and cold. Not that he gave a damn. He didn't want to sleep beside her anyway.

Liar! a voice in his head challenged. *You're as addicted to her as you are to smoking.*

"Oh, yeah?" he spoke to the voice out loud. "You don't see me puffing on a cigarette, do you?"

He didn't need a woman in his life, not a woman who kept lying to him, hurting him, making his heart go numb. He headed to the kitchen and poured himself another cup of coffee. Was it his third? His fourth? Maybe he ought to add a shot of brandy to it, just a little something to take the edge off. Michael shook his head. Caffeine, alcohol, tobacco. What the hell was wrong with him? Did he have to rely on a vice for everything?

He dumped the coffee in the sink, turned around and nearly tripped over his own booted feet.

Heather stood in the doorway, a long, flowing nightgown melting against her body like rose-colored wax.

"What are you doing?" he asked. Trying to haunt him?

She took a hesitant step. "I'm getting Justin a bottle."

"He's awake?"

She nodded. "His fever was up a little. I gave him something for it."

And now she would nurse him back to sleep, Michael thought. She was a good mother, tender and nurturing, but her maternal skills only made him ache.

The baby she'd carried in her womb had died. His baby. The child her brother had buried in a makeshift coffin.

She crossed to the refrigerator and filled a bottle. Michael wanted to bury his face in her hair and cry, mourn the way a father should be able to do. But he couldn't bring himself to touch her.

"How high is Justin's temperature?" he asked.

"A hundred and one."

"That sounds bad."

"Fevers tend to spike at night. He'll be okay. The medicine will start to work."

She capped the bottle, and Michael stared at her, wondering how she had looked all those months, swollen with his child.

Beautiful, he imagined.

"I better go," she said.

She turned away, and he drew a hard breath. "I'll go with you. I want to see Justin."

They entered the nursery together, careful not to touch, to brush shoulders, to make the slightest physical contact.

She lifted, the boy from his crib and settled onto the recliner, offering him the milk.

His little cheeks looked flushed, his pajama top askew. Heather righted the material, covering his tummy.

Michael stood beside the crib and listened to Justin suckle. Then he reached for the yellow pony and smoothed its gilded mane. "Was the other pony just like this one?" he asked.

Her voice was but a whisper. "Yes. It was identical."

He brought the stuffed toy to his face, touched it to his cheek, then took it away, unable to bear the softness. "Did it play the same music?"

"Yes." Again, a whisper. "The same lullaby."

Music that had taken their child to heaven, Michael thought. "Where is he buried? I need to know." He needed to see the site in his mind, to envision it.

"He was buried in the same place he was born. In Oklahoma. We were staying in a remote cabin in the

hills, a tiny place with a woodstove and log walls.''
She angled Justin's bottle, tipping it gently. The boy
was too tired to hold it himself, and the helplessness
made him seem younger, more infantlike. ''Reed laid
him to rest near a flowering tree. The blooms were
white, and when they fluttered to the ground, they
looked like wings.''

Michael didn't meet her gaze. He couldn't. He
knew her eyes were glossed with tears. He could hear
them in her voice, in her heart.

''I was going to tell you about him,'' she said.
''When things were stronger between us.''

He gave up, shifted, looked at her. ''Stronger?''

''I had dreams. Hopes. Foolish wishes.'' Moisture
beaded her lashes, shimmering like faceted jewels.
''Maybe he'll fall in love with me, maybe he'll commit to a future.''

''I did commit.'' He tried not to snarl, but his voice
still came out rough. ''We were becoming a family.''

''But you don't love me. How can we be a family
if you don't love me?''

Justin made an incoherent sound. He'd drunk half
of the milk, snuggling against Heather, tugging at the
ribbon on her nightgown, loosening the silk. Michael
envisioned her nursing a baby at her breast. Just as
quickly, he banished the image, refusing to let it take
root.

''Love isn't all it's cracked up to be,'' he said.

''How would you know?'' she challenged softy.

''I saw my mom suffer from it,'' he shot back just
as quietly.

At an impasse, they fell silent, words deadlocked
between them.

Justin nodded off. Heather carried him to the crib and tucked him in. Michael placed the yellow pony beside the boy and touched his forehead. His skin was cool, cooler than a hundred and one degrees.

"Justin is still my son," he said.

"I'm not trying to take him away from you."

Then why did he feel as if he were losing everything? The way he'd lost the other child?

He wanted to know what the boy had looked like, but he didn't have the heart to ask her to describe a dead baby. He glanced up and saw Heather watching him. Tears still speckled her lashes.

"You're going to leave, aren't you?" She'd promised to stay, but he knew she wouldn't keep that promise.

When she blinked, a teardrop fluttered without falling. "If you could only give me a reason to stay."

He shook his head, took a step back. She wanted him to love her, to let himself feel what he'd vowed to avoid. "I can't. I can't make it happen."

"I know." She wiped her eyes. "And I can't cry anymore. I can't dream, hope or wish." Reaching for the ribbon on her nightgown, she retied the bow. "I've hurt you deeply and I'm sorry for that. So terribly sorry. If I could undo the damage, I would."

But she couldn't, he thought.

And they both knew it was ending. Vanishing into the night, into a memory he would never forget.

The following day, Heather waited at Julianne and Bobby's door.

Julianne answered, wearing a sundress and a ponytail, looking bright and springy, stunning for her forty years.

"Hi," she said, flashing an Irish smile.

"Hi." Heather felt young and confused, eager for Julianne's wisdom. "Bobby isn't here, is he?"

"No, he took a tour group into the hills. Were you hoping to see him?"

"No, actually, it's you I came to see. But I thought it would be easier if we were alone. You know, girl talk."

"Then come in." Julianne reached for her hand, offering compassion already. "Where's Justin?" she asked, studying Heather's anxious expression.

"He isn't feeling well. Michael is with him." And she and Michael had barely spoken, not knowing what to say to each other this morning.

Julianne led her to the kitchen, directed her to the table and made two cups of tea. They sat across from each other, the sun beaming through the window, glinting off the appliances.

Baby Brendan slept nearby in a cradle-type swing, the *tick-tock* of the automatic motion lulling him into infant-sweet dreams.

Heather studied him for a moment, the way his fingers curled around the blanket, the way his tiny mouth puckered around a pacifier.

When she shifted her gaze, she caught Julianne watching her.

She couldn't tell the other woman about her stillborn baby. The child she'd nourished in her womb would always be her secret. Her heartache, her sadness. And now the grief was Michael's, as well.

Julianne tilted her head, her eyes as green as a never-ending meadow. "You look lost, Heather."

I am, she thought. Lost without the man I love. "Michael and I aren't going to make it. It's not going to work."

"Oh, sweetie. Are you sure?"

"Yes. It's over." She tasted her tea, but the honey-laced brew failed to warm the chill of rejection. "He's not in love with me. He never was."

"That's impossible." The freckles sprinkled across Julianne's nose twitched. "Have you seen the way he looks at you?"

"He cares. He's always cared. But it isn't love. He admitted as much."

"Oh, my." The other woman sat back. "I don't know what to say. You came to me for help, and I don't know what to say."

"It's okay. It helps just being here."

"Bobby and I had problems, too. I nearly left him. But in the end, he came through. He brought me into his life the way I needed him to. He shared his past with me. Everything about himself."

"I kept secrets from Michael, but he knows them now. He knows everything about me, the way you know everything about Bobby."

"Then give it some time," Julianne said.

"Time won't make him love me." She tried to let the motion of Brendan's swing relax her, to summon the strength to make a decision only she could make. "I'm going to move out. But I'm not sure where I should go."

"When I was prepared to leave, I chose to return home. To Pennsylvania, where I grew up." Julianne left her seat, opened a cupboard and retrieved a box of cookies. After lining a platter with vanilla-cream wafers, she placed them on the table. "Home is a good place to start."

Heather reached for a cookie, took a small bite. "Texas is my home. The Hill Country is where I grew up."

"I know." Julianne gave her a small smile.

"You think I should stay?"

"Yes, I do."

It was good advice, sound advice, logical advice, but Heather couldn't follow it.

Leaving Texas, and the fairy-tale wishes that went with it, was the only way to survive.

Heather returned to the farmhouse in a quiet mood. Michael expected as much. They didn't have much to say to each other. They seemed like strangers now.

Maybe they always had. Maybe there had been something missing all along, an ingredient Michael couldn't name.

Justin was awake, seated in his high chair, just as quiet as his parents. Did he sense something was wrong? Or was it the ear infection that kept him sullen?

"Hi, sweetheart." Heather smoothed the boy's thick dark hair, and he looked up and gave her a half-hearted smile. "Are you feeling better?"

"His fever broke," Michael said.

"You're fixing him lunch?" she asked.

It was a redundant question, considering the mashed and diced meal on the counter, but he figured it was the only thing she could think of to say.

"It's my day off. I don't mind staying home and being a dad." He set a shatterproof plate in front of Justin and let the boy pick at the finger foods.

Heather leaned against the counter. She looked tired. Pale yet pretty. She'd twisted her hair into a heavy bun on top of her head. Several long strands fell from the confinement, making Michael itch to tug all of it free.

She wore an embroidered blouse, tan trousers, a leather belt and boots to match. They were clothes from the past, articles he recognized, things she'd left behind when she'd disappeared.

"I need to make arrangements," she said.

He glanced at Justin, saw the boy squish a banana slice. "To leave?"

"Yes."

Michael froze. He knew this was coming. Yet the idea of losing her, of losing the child they'd agreed to raise, made fear claw like talons. His stomach went tight. A thorn pierced his chest. "Where are you going to go?" he asked.

"I don't know." Keeping busy, she began to load the dishwasher, clearing the dishes he'd left in the sink. "Somewhere. Anywhere."

Her response sounded distant, far removed from the family he'd thought they'd become.

"Julianne thinks I should stay in Texas. In this area." She scrubbed a plate, removing remnants from Michael's breakfast, pancakes he'd barely eaten. "But I can't. I don't belong here anymore. I need to start over."

He didn't want her to leave, but short of giving in

to the addiction, of losing his heart and what was left of his soul, he didn't know how to ask her to stay.

She closed the dishwasher and dried her hands. Somewhere along the way, she'd gotten a manicure. Her fingernails looked stronger, not nearly as brittle as the day she'd arrived.

"As soon as Justin is well enough to travel, I'll pick a place to go."

He envisioned her spinning a globe, choosing a new location at random. "You'll need money. Enough to keep you going until you find a job." He longed to take her in his arms, to hold her until the rest of the world disappeared. But that would only feed the obsession, make the ache inside him worse. "I'll help you get settled. In the meantime, you can stay here. In the guest room," he added.

"Thank you." When her voice turned raw, she cleared her throat.

He turned toward Justin. The boy had food all over his face, clumps of banana and peas on his bib and down the front of his pants.

What was he going to do without his son?

Be a long-distance dad, he told himself. Pay child support, send gifts, make phone calls, visit during holidays.

"Hey, buddy." He wiped the child's face and hands, receiving a frown for his effort.

"I'll give him a bath," Heather said.

Possessive, Michael reached for Justin. "I can do it."

Suddenly they stared at each other, tense and uncomfortable, like divorce-bound parents. How could this seem like the dissolution of a marriage? They'd never taken vows to begin with.

"Maybe we should do it together," he said, unable to cope with letting go this soon.

"Okay." Her voice was soft, sad. As lonely as the feeling sweeping over him.

They entered the bathroom, and she filled the tub, adding Justin's favorite bubble bath, two toy boats and a rubber octopus.

Mindful of Justin's illness, they kept him warm, sponging water over his body and washing him with a gentle cloth. The bathroom was cramped, the quarters near the tub tight. Justin seemed to enjoy having both parents at his beck and call. He gave the octopus a ride on the bigger boat and smiled at Mom and Dad.

It was strange to cherish one child while you mourned the other, Michael thought.

"I'm going to miss Justin's first birthday," he found himself saying. Surely Heather would be gone by then.

"I wish I could stay. But I can't. I just can't."

The rest of her words went unspoken. If Michael loved her, she would stay. But how could he? It hurt too much to give that deeply, to let someone steal your life's blood. He'd watched his mother die of cancer, but her spirit had died long before the disease had ravaged her. She'd perished from love, from the emotion that was supposed to heal.

Before the water cooled, Heather rinsed Justin and wrapped him in a towel. Fluffy and warm, he clung to her, handing Michael the octopus.

"Thanks, buddy." He had the urge to keep it, to

tuck it away somewhere, to hold it against his heart when the child was gone.

Should he keep something of Heather's, too? Her favorite perfume? A jeweled hair barrette? The pearl choker he'd given her on her twentieth birthday?

No, not the pearls. He couldn't take back a gift.

He followed Heather into the nursery and watched her diaper and dress the baby.

When she looked up, their eyes met.

His friend.

His former lover.

The lady, heaven help him, he simply couldn't keep.

Twelve

Michael sat at his desk in the office he shared with his uncle at the barn, unable to concentrate. Bobby kept sliding him sideways glances, making him moodier than he already was.

"You okay, Mike?"

He shrugged and riffled through his desk drawer, taking inventory: a box of pens, two candy bars, a self-inking rubber stamp, a scatter of paper clips, a pocket calendar, scissors, a stack of Elk Ridge Ranch catalogs. Digging a little deeper, he found a crumpled, half-empty pack of cigarettes.

Tempted to light one up, he frowned. No doubt they were stale by now.

Bobby spoke again, cutting into the silence, cutting into Michael's heart. "You're missing Heather already."

"She isn't gone yet." He loosened a cigarette from

the pack, broke it in half and watched the tobacco litter his drawer.

"You're still missing her."

"She's been part of my life since I was a kid." And six days had passed since she'd decided to leave. Justin was nearly well enough to travel, so it was only a matter of time before she packed up the boy and left.

She was considering relocating to Oregon or Washington, maybe Northern California. She'd promised to keep in touch, of course. But that didn't ease the emptiness.

Was this how his mom had felt when she'd lost his dad? When he'd walked away, leaving her pregnant with his child?

Michael turned to face his uncle. "Why didn't my mom ever get over my dad?"

Reacting to the change of topic, Bobby shifted in his chair. "Your mother didn't talk to me about your father. We didn't discuss him, not to any degree. She was concerned about you, Mike. About what was going to happen to you."

Which made sense, he supposed. His mom had been terminally ill when she'd contacted Bobby, when she'd asked him to take care of his brother's son.

"So she never told you that my dad was the love of her life?"

"No." Bobby shook his head. "She barely mentioned Cameron. But he'd been dead for quite a while by then."

Michael nodded. Cameron Elk, the father he'd never met, had been killed in a bar fight many years before. "Did you know she kept scrapbooks about him? Rodeo clippings and such?"

Surprised, Bobby lifted his brows. "No, I didn't. Do you still have them? Or did you get rid of them after she died?"

"I still have them." Yellowed pages, he thought. Faded photographs of a prominent cowboy. "I knew they were important to my mom."

"She was a nice lady."

"Yes, she was." Michael pictured her, with her blond hair and blue eyes, her soft-spoken nature. She'd met his dad at the local diner where she'd worked, and whenever he'd been on his way to a rodeo in the area, he would spend the night at her house. But after he'd discovered that she'd conceived his child, he never came back.

Bobby frowned. "I'm sorry about what my brother did. Cameron had no right to abandon you."

"It wasn't so bad. I got lucky. I got you." He gazed at the man who'd kept him from being completely orphaned, who'd relocated to Texas to raise him. "The tough part for me is thinking about my mom. All those years she waited for my dad to come back, that she believed in him. Being in love kept her from being truly happy."

Bobby's frown grew more intense, more troubled. "Being in love isn't what kept her from being happy. Being alone is what hurt." He came around to the side of his desk and sat on the edge of it. "How would you feel if you never saw Heather again?"

Restless, Michael snapped another cigarette in half. "I didn't see her for eighteen months."

"I know. But deep down, you hoped she would come back. A part of you didn't let go."

"I'm letting go now."

"But why?" Bobby asked. "Heather isn't treating you the way Cameron treated your mom. She loves you, Michael."

"It isn't that simple." He closed his drawer, shutting out the scattered tobacco. "There are things you don't understand. Things I can't explain. Besides, I'll see her again. We have a son together. We'll be in touch for the rest of our lives."

Or would they? What if Heather wasn't happy in Oregon or Washington or wherever she went? What if she considered a monumental change?

What if she called the FBI and asked them to bring her and the baby into the Witness Protection Program with Reed?

Michael would lose her and Justin forever. His woman and his child would no longer exist. Their identities would change, and his family would be lost.

Panicked, he shoved away from his desk, then stood on wobbly legs, suddenly desperate to see Heather.

"I'm going home for a while," Michael said.

Without waiting for a response, he exited the barn, climbed into his truck and drove to the farmhouse.

He found Heather at the dining-room table, typing her résumé on a laptop, a computer they had always shared. Her half-eaten lunch sat nearby, the crust on a chicken-salad sandwich picked away and discarded on the side of the dish.

He assumed Justin was down for his nap, sleeping on this quiet afternoon.

As Michael shifted his feet, she looked over her shoulder, then turned back to her work, avoiding his gaze.

When they were kids, he used to tug on her hair to get her attention. But they weren't kids anymore, he thought. And a playful tug would only make him ache.

What was he doing here? Torturing himself?

She reached for her soda, and he watched her hand curl around the can. As she took a sip, he moved closer, hovering like a vulture.

Should he admit that he could barely eat? Barely sleep? Barely survive without her? God help him, but he longed to touch her again, to inhale her scent, to absorb the texture of her skin, the beat of her pulse.

"I'm worried about something," he said, coming around the table so she could see him.

She set her soda down. "What?"

"That you'll disappear. That you'll enter the Witness Protection Program with Reed, and I'll never see you or Justin again." It was a plausible scenario, he thought. Much too plausible. The mob wouldn't suspect that Justin was Reed's son, not if Heather was with the boy. "You'd be gone for good."

"I would never do that." She pushed her chair back a little. "As much as I miss my brother, I'd miss you more. I couldn't imagine not ever seeing you again, not keeping in touch by phone or—"

"Don't leave me, Heather." He blurted the words, his heartbeat blasting his chest. "Please, don't leave."

Stunned, she gazed at him. He sat next to her, doing his damnedest to regain his composure, to handle this without falling apart.

"Why?" she asked, putting him on the spot. "Why should I stay?"

"Because I'm—" Anxious, apprehensive, he

paused. Once he said the words, once he acknowledged his feelings out loud, there was no turning back.

"You're what?" she pressed.

"In love with you." Not obsessed or addicted. In love, he thought.

Her eyes widened and her voice turned wary. "Since when?"

He thought back to their youth, to the day she'd asked him to marry her, to wrap a Cherokee blanket around their shoulders and take a private vow. "Since you were sixteen, and I was too old to have you."

"You called me jailbait."

"I wanted you. More than you can imagine. For a moment, I even considered your offer."

"My offer?" Her voice quavered. "The secret ceremony?"

He nodded, reached for her hand. "Does it still stand?"

Her hand trembled in his. "You want to marry me?"

"Yes, but not in secret. I want a public wedding, with friends and family, and—"

Her eyes watered, fogged with disbelief. "Oh, Michael. Are you sure?"

"Yes." He understood his feelings now, the way he'd confused love with loneliness. "I don't want to live without you. I was afraid to admit how much I needed you. But I'm not afraid anymore." But he was still nervous, he thought. Dizzy from the truth, from the admission of love.

She left her chair and came to him, slipping her arms around his shoulders, calming him. He rose, and in the light of day, they gazed at each other. He didn't repeat his question, asking if she still wanted to be his wife. He could see the answer in her eyes.

Heather reached for the buttons on his shirt and undid them, one by one. She needed to strip away the pain from the past, to press her cheek against his heart and make a new memory.

Michael Elk loved her. And he always had.

"I gave up on dreams." On wishing wells, shooting stars and fairy tales, she thought. On hope for the future.

He kept her close. "So did I. But I won't, not ever again."

"Me, neither." His chest rose and fell, strong and steady against her cheek. "How did you know, Michael? What made you realize that you love me?"

He kissed the top of her head, encouraging her to look up at him. "It was something my uncle said. He asked me how I would feel if I never saw you again. And then suddenly I was panicking about losing you for good."

"I'm here to stay," she told him. "I'll never go away again."

"I'm sorry I hurt you," he whispered. "That I denied how I felt about you."

"I'm sorry, too." She'd never meant to end up on the run, to leave him steeped in fear.

"You've apologized enough, Heather. It's time to move on."

Guilt clenched her heart. "But our baby didn't survive. If I'd been in a hospital, if I'd—"

"Shh." He smoothed a hand down her hair, comforting her. "It wasn't your fault."

Sadness swirled in her mind. "I should have given him a name."

"No." He shook his head. "You did the right thing. You followed the old Cherokee way." He paused, took a deep breath. "Will you take me to the place he's buried?"

"Yes." She understood that he needed to say goodbye to the child he'd never known, to the infant she'd cradled in her womb.

When they both fell silent, he led her to their bedroom and kissed her, starting the day over, refreshing his confession of love.

She took what he offered, lost in the beauty of magic, of silver-wrapped wishes and floral-scented dreams. Roaming his body, she paused to unbuckle his belt and unfasten his jeans. He backed her toward the bed, and they eased their way onto the sheets, undressing each other, hands and mouths questing.

Sensation slid over sensation, and pleasure, sweet wicked pleasure, welcomed need. Their lips met, softly, slowly, setting a languid rhythm.

She closed her eyes, then opened them, watching him caress the swell of her breasts, his tongue darting to taste, to tease, to make the moment last.

As the sun lit the shadows on his face, and his hair draped her in a dark, almost dangerous curtain, she knew this was Michael—the boy who'd charmed her with his smile, the rough, hard-edged man who'd molded and shaped her life.

Their eyes met, and he rose above her, determined to give her more, to take her higher, to make the girl she had once been, the woman she'd become, fall in love all over again.

Michael, Heather and Justin arrived in Oklahoma on a dry, hot afternoon. The road to the cabin was a

SHERI WHITEFEATHER 179

long, rough trek, a path flanked by rock formations and foliage.

This wasn't the familiar terrain of Michael's homeland, but it was still beautiful. The ground was speckled with grass, trees and little yellow flowers that grew like weeds.

When the cabin came into view, he gazed at the primitive wooden structure. The tiny log dwelling appeared to be unoccupied, a lone building that rarely received tenants. But it was, he supposed, too far from civilization to provide the comfort most folks were looking for.

He glanced at Heather. She sat beside him in the rented SUV, as golden as the flowers that dotted the land.

She smiled at him, and his heart turned as warm as wax, melting like a candle. He knew this was difficult for her, coming back to the place where she'd birthed and buried a child. But she was here for him, the father of that lost child.

He parked near the cabin, and Justin awakened in the back seat, stretching and moaning.

"Are you ready?" Michael asked Heather.

She nodded, and they exited the vehicle. He unbuckled Justin from his car seat and lifted the boy into his arms. Justin clung to him, still battling sleep. He smoothed the child's thick dark hair and moved closer to Heather.

"It's this way," she said, guiding them past the rustic building and into a wooded area that stretched for miles.

They weaved in and out of peeling bark and greenery, then suddenly Michael saw the tree that marked the baby's grave. It rose from the ground like an angel, its summer blooms as white and fluffy as feathers.

As they approached, Justin made an awed sound. Michael's eyes went misty.

With Heather at his side, they knelt beneath the tree. Michael sat Justin in front of him and let the boy cup a handful of the fallen blooms.

"There was another baby," Heather told Justin. "And we're here to say goodbye to him."

"He had a pony just like yours," Michael added.

"Pa?" The child looked up. He was nearing his first birthday, his little legs growing sturdier. Soon he would be walking, then running through the grass at home.

"The other baby was our son," Michael went on. "But you're our son, too." The child of their heart, he thought. The sweet, beautiful boy they would love and cherish for the rest of their lives.

Justin handed Michael one of the white petals and he took it willingly, holding it like a snowflake in the palm of his hand.

This would be the first and only time they would mention the other baby to Justin. Heather's brother had asked them to keep Justin's true parentage a secret and that meant keeping the existence of the infant who'd died a secret as well.

Heather smoothed her hand over the ground. "Beverly is with him," she said. "We're watching over her baby, and she's watching over ours."

Michael nodded. His eyes were watering again, but he didn't want to cry. He didn't want this moment to be sad.

Making peace with his emotions, he kissed

Heather's cheek. She put her head on his shoulder, and for a while they remained silent.

Finally, he recited a Cherokee prayer his uncle had taught him long ago. While he spoke the words, Justin settled onto his lap, listening to the language of their ancestors.

Afterward, Michael said goodbye to the other baby and reached for Heather's hand.

It was time to go home, he thought. To marry the woman he loved and raise the child the Creator had given them.

He came to his feet and as he turned to leave, with his family by his side, a small breeze blew, fluttering leaves on the white-blossomed tree and scattering them joyously beneath the sun.

Beneath the glow of a perfect summer day.

Epilogue

Heather had waited for this moment all her life. Didn't most little girls dream about their wedding day? Plan the ceremony in their minds?

She stood in front of a full-length mirror in the bridal-party dressing room, gazing at her reflection. A sleeveless gown flowed to her ankles in a pool of white, the bodice adorned with colorful ribbon and tiny beads. She wore her hair long and loose, the way Michael liked it best.

''You look radiant.'' Julianne came up behind her, her tone soft and genuine.

''Thank you.'' She had chosen Julianne as her matron of honor, and the other woman's presence gave her a warm and welcome sense of family.

As happy as Heather was, she missed Beverly and her brother. But Reed would be all right, she told herself. He had a chance to start over, to search for peace.

"Are you ready?" Julianne asked.

She met the redhead's gaze in the mirror. "I'm more than ready." To marry the man she loved, to spend the rest of her life with Michael Damian Elk.

Julianne handed Heather her bouquet, an arrangement of roses and wildflowers.

They took the path to the wedding site, where summer blooms flourished around a redwood gazebo. Heather wanted to get married at the ranch, with the hills shimmering in the distance and the setting sun painting the sky a brilliant hue.

She spotted Michael at the altar, dressed in a colorful Cherokee-style shirt, a blue blanket draped around his shoulders, signifying his old life and ways, a tradition in his culture.

"I'm so pleased for both of you." This came from Bobby, who stood nearby, waiting to give Heather away.

"Thank you." She turned to the groom's uncle. He held Justin in his arms, and the boy reached out to hug her.

She kissed her son and watched Bobby set the boy on the ground, where he stood proudly on his own.

As the music began and Julianne started down the floral-lined aisle, passing misty-eyed guests, Heather beamed. Julianne held Justin's hand, and the little one toddled along, taking excited steps, bouncing the way babies did when they finally learned to walk.

Maria, who stood in for mother-of-the-bride, was at the altar too, rocking baby Brendan and watching Justin swing a satin pillow in his free hand.

Bobby draped Heather with a blue blanket like the

one Michael wore, and soon she was gliding toward the groom. They had decided to blend their cultures, to create a ceremony that was uniquely theirs.

When she stood beside him, he smiled. Her heart pounded in her chest, awed by the sight of him, by the love and admiration in his gaze.

The minister said a prayer, asking the Creator to give Heather and Michael a long and happy life together.

After they said their vows, they exchanged rings. Next, they drank from a double-side vase, a piece of pottery made just for this occasion.

When the vase was broken and the pieces scattered into the earth, Heather and Michael became one.

A white blanket was placed around their shoulders, bringing them closer. The final Cherokee tradition, she thought as he leaned in to kiss her.

The blanket that sealed their union.

That made Heather's dream of being Michael's wife, the woman who captured his heart, come true.

*   *   *   *   *

*Look for Sheri WhiteFeather's next
Silhouette Desire,*

THE HEART OF A STRANGER,

part of the

LONE STAR COUNTRY CLUB

in-line continuity available this August.

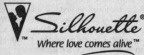

COMING NEXT MONTH

#1525 THE LIBRARIAN'S PASSIONATE KNIGHT—
Cindy Gerard
Dynasties: The Barones
Love was the last thing on Daniel Barone's mind…until he rescued
Phoebe Richards from her pushy ex one fateful night. The shy librarian
was undeniably appealing, with her delectable curves and soft brown eyes, but
had this sexy bachelor finally met the woman who'd tame his playboy heart?

#1526 BILLIONAIRE BACHELORS: GRAY—
Anne Marie Winston
After Gray MacInnes underwent a heart transplant, he began having
flashes of strange memories…which led him to his donor's elegant widow,
Catherine Thorne, and her adorable son. His memories of endless nights
with her in his arms soon became a breathtaking reality, but Gray only
hoped Catherine would forgive him once she learned his true identity.

#1527 THE HEART OF A STRANGER—Sheri WhiteFeather
Lone Star Country Club
When she found a handsome stranger unconscious on her ranch,
Lourdes Quinterez had no idea her life was about to change forever.
She nursed the man back to health only to learn he had amnesia. Though
Juan Guapo, as she called him, turned out to be Ricky Mercado, former
mob boss, Lourdes would stand by the man who'd melted her heart with his
smoldering kisses.

#1528 LONETREE RANCHERS: BRANT—Kathie DeNosky
Never able to resist a woman in need, bullfighter Brant Wakefield was happy
to help lovely heiress Annie Devereaux when she needed protection from a
dangerous suitor. But soon they were falling head over heels for each other, and
though Brant feared they were too different to make it work, his passion for her
would not be denied.…

#1529 DESERT WARRIOR—Nalini Singh
Family pressure had forced Mina Coleridge to reject her soul mate four
years ago. Now circumstances had brought Tariq Zamanat back to her—as
her husband! Though he shared his body with her, his heart was considered
off-limits. But Mina had lost Tariq once before, and *this* time she was
determined to hold on to her beloved sheik.

#1530 HAVING THE TYCOON'S BABY—Anna DePalo
The Baby Bank
All Liz Donovan needed to realize her dream of having a baby was a trip
to the fertility clinic. But then the unthinkable happened—her teenage crush,
millionaire Quentin Whittaker, proposed a marriage of convenience! It wasn't
long before Liz was wondering if making a baby the old-fashioned way could
lead to the family of her dreams.

SDCNM0703